# SHADOWS OF DECEPTION

## DI SARA RAMSEY
### BOOK 27

## M A COMLEY

# ACKNOWLEDGMENTS

Special thanks as always go to @studioenp for their superb cover design expertise.

My heartfelt thanks go to my wonderful editor Emmy, my proofreaders Joseph and Barbara for spotting all the lingering nits.

A special shoutout to all my wonderful ARC Group, who help to keep me sane.

*To my mother, gone but never forgotten. Miss you every second of every day, Mum.*

*My heart is breaking a second time with the loss of Dex, my beloved pup. But Tilly is healing it slowly.*

# PROLOGUE

The office felt stuffier than usual. Richard left his seat, turned down the thermostat on his radiator, then returned to his desk. He glanced up at the clock. It was five forty-five. A knock on the door drew his attention. "Come in," he bellowed.

His secretary, Barbara, stuck her head into the room. "I'm off now, Mr Manning. Unless you'd like me to hang around until your last appointment has been and gone?"

"Nonsense. You get off to your family. Is everyone else leaving now?"

"Yes. In fact, most of them have left already. They were very eager to get home tonight."

"Good for them. I'd be inclined to do the same if Elizabeth were home this evening. As you know, she's off into town to see that new show at the theatre with her friends."

"I hope she has a lovely time. I've heard it's very good, although, it wouldn't be my cup of tea."

"Nor mine. Each to their own, eh? You go home and enjoy yourself. Will hubby have your dinner on the table?"

Barbara snorted, then covered her mouth out of embarrassment. She dropped her hand and grinned. "Hell would have to freeze over before he did that, sir. Now, when it comes to turning food on the barbecue, well, he's a dab hand at doing that. Not a job I enjoy, so that's fine by me."

"Ah, yes. It's pretty much the same in my house. Although, I can manage to knock up a decent roast when Elizabeth isn't in the mood for cooking, which, in fairness, isn't that often, despite her meeting up with friends for lunch now and again."

Barbara smiled. "I'll see you in the morning, then. Maybe you should leave your office door open for now. That way you can hear when Mr Bullman arrives. Just to remind you, he's due at six-fifteen. Enjoy the rest of your evening when you finally get home."

"Thank you. I'll see you in the morning."

Barbara left the door ajar, and he got back to completing the paperwork he had set aside during the day, aware that his hours would be extended.

It wasn't long before he found himself distracted by a new case that had come his way in the last few days. So much so that he neglected to hear Mr Bullman arrive until he knocked on his office door. Richard jumped out of his seat and crossed the room to shake his hand. "Sorry, I was miles away. Come in. How are you, Mr Bullman?"

"Please, call me Laurence. *Mr Bullman* is reserved for my father."

Both men laughed.

"Take a seat. Sorry, I can't offer you a coffee. My secretary, Barbara, is very particular about who uses her coffee machine, and I've caused a disaster or two in the past when I've tinkered with it."

Laurence waved away his apology. "There's no need. To tell you the truth, I'm looking forward to having a swift one at the pub after our meeting."

Richard retook his seat and smiled. "Sounds like a super idea to me. My wife is out this evening, so now that you've put the thought in my head, I might nip to my local on my way home, too."

"We deserve to unwind at the end of a long day. I can't thank you enough for agreeing to see me today. It's so hard getting away from the office during the day, especially when you're self-employed."

"As long as this is a one-off. I'm always keen to help a prospective client out of a hole. You mentioned that you'd been in a car accident. Why don't you give me the details of what happened?"

"I was out with a friend. Actually, I was giving him a lift home from the office as his car was in the local garage for repairs. Anyway, we approached this junction at a roundabout. I took the right-hand lane to go straight ahead of me, and this idiot cut me up and switched lanes halfway round. He took the front bumper off and left my wheel buckled. I managed to limp to the side of the road until the AA appeared."

"Sounds nasty. Did the driver stop?"

"Yes. He pulled over but started ranting at me, saying it was my fault for being in the right hand lane."

"How ridiculous. What happened to your car?"

"It was towed to my local garage. I had to fork out for a taxi that night. The insurer is claiming that the driver of the other vehicle hasn't done anything wrong. Now I'm saddled with repairs of over two thousand pounds, which I can't afford."

"What utter nonsense. Well, don't worry, it sounds like an open-and-shut case to me. Your insurance firm is in the wrong. They should be footing the bill. That's what they're there for."

"Phew, what a relief. I thought I was up shit creek for a moment there. Where do we go from here?"

"If you write down the name of your insurance and your other details for me, I can start working on the case first thing in the morning."

"And I'll have your fees on top."

"Of course. I won't charge you much. It should only take a letter from me to resolve the issue. Insurers despise it when solicitors become involved."

Richard slipped a notebook across the desk, and Laurence scribbled down the relevant information and slid the notebook back.

"That's great. Leave it with me. I'll be in touch with you in a few days. I'll show you out."

They left their seats. Laurence noticed his shoelace was undone and dropped to one knee to tie it. By this time, Richard was already standing by the door.

"Always best to tie them up rather than faceplant the pavement in the street," Richard jested.

Bullman smiled and jumped to his feet. "Sorry about the delay."

Richard turned his back and walked towards the main door, until he felt an arm around his throat.

"Oh no you don't." Bullman dragged Richard back into his office and slammed the door shut behind them.

Fear shot through him. His hands wrapped around Bullman's arm, trying to loosen the man's suffocating grip. He coughed, choked and spluttered, "Please, you're hurting me. Let's talk about this."

"Nothing to talk about. It's all about the money for you. Your type has no feelings for the average person walking the streets, do you? Money-grabbing fuckers. Every solicitor is the same. But here's some news for you: that's not what this is about."

Richard was hauled across the room to his chair and forced to sit. Bullman quickly bound his arms behind his back before Richard had the chance to realise what was going on. For the first time in his life, he didn't know what to say to get out of the situation. To his knowledge, he'd never met this man before.

After Richard's arms were bound tightly, Bullman appeared in front of him, holding what looked like a hunting knife. He played with the blade, running his finger up and down it, and narrowed his eyes as he stared at Richard.

"Just tell me what you want. There's no need for all of this. I'm willing to listen to any grievances you have. Is it something I've done to you? Are you upset with the way one of the other solicitors has treated you? Let me make amends if they have. Give me the opportunity to right the wrong that has made you angry. We can work it out together if you're willing to trust me."

"Trust you? Don't make me laugh. You're evil personified because of what you did."

Richard frowned. "Because of what I did? Sorry, I don't understand. You're going to have to spell it out for me."

Bullman smiled and wiggled his eyebrows. "Now there's a thought. What an exceptionally good idea for you to come up with at the most stressful time of your life. Right, where shall we do this?" He swiped the pen tidy, phone and letter racks to the floor.

Richard stared down at his possessions, wondering what the hell Bullman was going to do next.

Then Bullman took the knife and, starting from the left-hand corner, carved the words 'The truth is in the shadows' into the mahogany desk, which had been commissioned for Richard five years ago at a cost of over ten thousand pounds.

"I don't understand. What does that mean?"

Bullman sneered and leaned forward. "Don't pretend you don't know. Have the courage of your convictions before you meet your Maker."

"What? I genuinely haven't got a clue what you're talking about. Please enlighten me."

"The time for talking was over long ago. You've walked free from your crimes for decades. The time has come for the judge and jury to decide your fate. Umm... that's me, by the way."

Richard shook his head repeatedly. "I'm sorry, I don't understand. I've done nothing wrong. I'm a man of honour. I think you've made a mistake. You've got the wrong Richard Manning. I know there are several men with the same name as me in the area. Let me talk to them. We can get all this sorted within a few minutes, but first, you're going to need to untie me."

"Don't try to fool me. I know what you're guilty of. You're going to pay for what you did to those people."

"People? What people? I genuinely don't know what you're talking about."

Bullman ran his finger along the length of the blade again, careful not to cut himself. Then he took a step forward, looked Richard in the eye and said, "Is there anything else you'd like to add before I put an end to this charade?"

"What... what do you mean? Put an end to it? I swear I haven't done anything wrong."

Bullman tutted, put his finger under Richard's chin and lifted his head slightly. "You had your chance. You screwed up."

Richard felt the blade slice through his throat. Blood filled his mouth, and his eyes widened with fear as he gasped for breath. Then he was left with the image of his wife and son swimming in his mind before his eyes closed for the final time. Bullman's laughter could be heard in the distance.

# 1

Sara kissed her husband, Mark, farewell before they jumped into their respective vehicles. He had a long day ahead of him at his own veterinary practice, and Sara, a Detective Inspector in the West Mercia Police Force, really didn't know what to expect from one day to the next. Cases were coming in thick and fast, varied this year, and they weren't even halfway through it. She switched on her radio to catch the latest news. The newscaster revealed that a criminal her team had been responsible for catching in their last case was due to appear in court, along with her former boss, DCI Carol Price.

She'd struggled to rid herself of the image of confronting her boss and the subsequent slap on the back she had received from the superintendent. She hadn't wanted things to turn out that way but, thankfully, Sara had morals and was always keen to stick to the rule book. She was also reeling from the notion that her boss had been betraying her for years. Something that she hadn't had an inkling about since she'd been working alongside Price. Now, because of her greed, Price was about to be hauled before the court and punished for being the corrupt officer Sara and her team had exposed her to be.

A horn blasted behind her. She waved an apology at the frustrated driver and pulled out of the junction that would lead her into the city. The traffic was lighter than normal. She had realised quickly that leaving home ten minutes earlier was always the key to a less stressful start to her day. She parked in her space just as her partner, Detective Sergeant Carla Jameson, pulled up alongside her. Sara smiled, but Carla seemed distracted and was talking to someone on her phone. She waited patiently for her partner to finish.

"Hey, is everything all right? You seem worked up about something."

Carla closed her eyes and gritted her teeth. Her head shook with rage. "Bloody caterers—they're doing my head in. I've told them what we want for our wedding day, and now they're telling us that the salmon is in short supply."

"What? The wedding isn't for another three weeks. Why can't they get another supplier?"

"Exactly. That's what I just asked. The bloke started talking to me as if I were a child."

"Can't you go with another caterer?"

"No, it's too late. They know they've got me by the short and curlies. I knew we should have eloped. I wanted to, but Des was determined he wanted the works and then took a step back and insisted I should deal with it."

Sara had to bite her tongue. She wasn't one for interfering in people's relationships, although she'd had to break that rule a few times over the years where Carla was concerned.

"What? Don't you have any wise words to offer?"

Sara wagged a finger. "Here are some for you: don't take your foul mood out on me."

Carla winced and bashed the side of her head with her fist. "Sorry. I didn't mean to. Why does all the organising have to fall on the woman's shoulders? It's so unfair."

"I agree, it shouldn't. Maybe it's a reminder of what's to come."

"Meaning?" Carla asked.

They walked towards the main entrance.

"Meaning you have a lot to learn about relationships and married life if you believe it's going to be fifty-fifty."

Carla grumbled and opened the front door. "That sucks. I work as hard as Des, if not harder. If he thinks I'm going to roll over and do everything around the house when we get married, he's got another think coming."

Sara placed a hand over her chest and said, "You mean you haven't sat down and held the dreaded conversation yet?"

Carla bit her lip. "No. Do you think it's too late?" she asked seriously.

Sara laughed and elbowed her partner. "I'm pulling your leg. Mind you, maybe it's something you should find time to discuss if you feel that strongly about it." She waved at the desk sergeant and punched her security code into the keypad.

"Enough about me. Today is the day, isn't it?"

"If you mean the day the new DCI starts his job, then yes. I've just heard on the news that Carol Price is also appearing in court later today."

"I still can't believe she was able to dupe everyone at the station for the past ten to fifteen years. It's sickening."

"*Duped* is the right word. I feel the onus is on me for not seeing through her."

"Bollocks. What are you talking about? You didn't live in her pocket day in, day out. We concentrate fully on our investigations. How often did you chat with her?"

"I know, but I've always prided myself on being a good judge of character. What happened with the DCI? I didn't have an inkling. I had no suspicion at all that something was wrong."

"You, along with everyone else at the station, Sara. You can't spend the rest of your life blaming yourself."

"Can't I? It's going to affect my decision-making going forward—it has to."

"It needn't. You should regard it as a blip on your radar that you found and deleted. End of."

"As easy as that, eh?"

They entered the incident room. As usual, they were the first to arrive. Carla switched on most of the computers while Sara made them both a coffee.

"I'm going to crack on with sorting through my post. I have a feeling DCI Blake will call me into his office, probably at nine on the dot."

"What do you know about him?"

"I've carried out my due diligence. He seems all right, but then, so did Carol Price, and we both know how that turned out, don't we?"

"He's from Devon, isn't he?"

"Yes, he was based in Exeter. I have an old colleague down that way. He did some digging for me and didn't find anything on his record, except for a couple of parking tickets."

"That's good. Makes a change."

"We'll see. I'm not sure how I feel working under a man again."

Carla chuckled and raised her eyebrows. "So to speak."

Sara shook her head. "I'm going if you can't have a conversation without it sinking to the gutter." She turned on her heel and marched into her office.

Carla appeared in the doorway, waving a white tissue. "Sorry. I was only joking."

"That makes two of us," Sara said. "Let me know when the rest of the team arrive. In the meantime, can you go over the paperwork from the last case and make sure everything that needs to be filed is sorted?"

"If I have to."

"You do, unless you want to swap with me."

Carla backed out of the room. "Umm... I hear the file calling my name. Good luck." She closed the door behind her.

Sara sat at her desk and sipped her drink while she tore open all the envelopes lying in her in-tray. In between, she booted up her computer and opened her email account. "Damn, I wish I hadn't done that." Fifteen important emails sat in her inbox, vying for attention. She swivelled her screen away from her and dealt with the post first.

At nine on the dot, she received the call she was expecting. "DI Ramsey? This is DCI Blake. I'd like you to report to my office within the next ten minutes."

"I'll be there, sir."

"Good. I look forward to meeting you."

He abruptly ended the call before she could say anything else. Sara shuffled her papers together and shoved them back into her in-tray. She gave her emails a cursory glance, deciding they could wait until she had a spare half an hour at the end of the day. Then she joined the rest of the team for a brief morning meeting, which mainly involved going over old ground on the case they'd just completed. "Let's crack on with it. I'd like it all done and dusted by the end of the day, folks. My stomach is stirring, and we all know what that means."

"That you have wind from the curry you had last night," Craig offered, ever the joker.

"I'll ignore that comment. Okay, I've been summoned to meet the new chief. Wish me luck."

Carla stepped forward and gave her a quick hug. "That's for courage. You'll be fine. If anything, that's probably what's giving your stomach the jitters."

"I'm not so sure. If anything comes in, don't hesitate to give me a shout. In fact, please make up an excuse to come and get me if I'm not back within half an hour."

Carla laughed. "Deal. We're all intrigued to know what he's like. Make sure you grill him as much as he's probably going to grill you."

"Oh God, don't say that. I hate being grilled by a senior officer." Sara left the incident room and marched along the corridor to the chief's office.

Mary, the former DCI's loyal secretary, greeted her with a smile.

"How are you, Mary?"

"As well as can be expected. I don't think I'll ever get over the shock of finding out Price was corrupt. I thought I knew that woman well; how wrong I was. I swear I didn't have an inkling she was bent; otherwise, I would have raised a concern with you."

"That's good to hear. You're not alone; she fooled all of us. Let's try and strike that from our memories now." Sara gestured with her head towards the chief's door. "What's he like?" she whispered.

Mary nodded. "So far so good. He laid the ground rules down with me as soon as he arrived, which was ten minutes before he was due to start. Of course, I was already here, fortunately. We'll have to see how it goes. If for some reason it doesn't work out, I'll move on. Secretarial jobs are easy to come by, or at least, they used to be. I haven't checked in a while; I haven't felt the necessity to. Sorry, I'm rambling and taking up too much of your time. I'll bring you through a cup of coffee in a moment. Oh, wait, I'd better introduce you. Sorry, my head is all over the place today. I'm keen to make a good impression from the start."

Sara touched Mary's forearms. "Hey, stop working yourself up into a state. Neither of us has to prove anything to him. We're both honest and hardworking. That should be enough for any new boss to appreciate."

"Thanks, I needed to hear that, Inspector Ramsey." She smiled and knocked on her boss's door. He bellowed for her to enter. She opened it and said, "Sorry to interrupt, sir. DI Ramsey is here to see you."

"Thank you, Mary. If you would be so kind as to show her in."

Mary stood back, allowing Sara to enter the room. "I'll make some coffee for you both."

"That would be splendid. Come in, Inspector Ramsey. I've been eager to meet you. Take a seat."

His hair was virtually grey. Sara estimated his age to be in his late forties. He had lines around his eyes. His skin was tanned as if he'd just returned from a holiday, probably to the Caribbean. Her gaze dropped to his desk, where a silver frame displayed a photo of a woman and two teenage boys. Sara took a seat opposite him, unsure whether she should offer her hand before she sat down or not.

"I sense you're a little on edge, Inspector. Why don't we ditch the formalities and cut to the chase?"

"If that's what you'd prefer, sir. I'm not on edge as such, just a tad wary, I suppose, after what happened with your predecessor."

"Which is totally understandable. I appreciate what a shock to the system that must have been to you and your team, not forgetting poor Mary out there. I'm aware it's going to take time to build up a trust between us, but I'm willing to give it a go. The question is, are you?"

"Of course, sir. It has been a tough few weeks around here for the staff, getting to grips with what went on with Price. I had always got on well with her. She gave me no reason to distrust her. That's the hard part in all of this."

"Hey, you mustn't blame yourself. Don't forget, she managed to pull the wool over her senior officers' eyes as well."

"I keep trying to tell myself that, sir, but I suppose I worked more closely with her than any of them, and... it hurts, in all honesty. I've always given my all to the job, and for her to betray my trust..."

"There's no need for you to continue that sentence. I get it, honestly, I do. Let's not talk about her. She'll have her day in court, and we'll both be there to see her get the justice she deserves. I want to hear all about you."

"There's not really that much to tell, sir. I arrived here around seven years ago. I was transferred from Liverpool. I needed to get away after my husband was killed."

"I'm sorry to hear that. Was he a serving police officer?"

"No. He ran his own metal-working business. We were due to meet up for lunch as he had taken an unexpected trip into town. He ended up being shot by gang members." She lowered her head as sudden tears clouded her vision. "I'm sorry, it's still painful to talk about."

"I'm sure it is. Let's leave it there then. What brought you south to Hereford?"

"My parents live here, well, my father does. We lost Mum a couple of years ago. Another tough moment in my life."

"It sucks at times, doesn't it? The older we get, the tougher it seems to be on us. How is your father holding up?"

She smiled. "He's doing well. Thank you for asking. He's met a wonderful lady called Margaret. I think we'll be getting an invite to a wedding soon."

He smiled, and it seemed to be genuine. "That's lovely to hear. Send them both my best wishes." His gaze dropped to her hands. "I see a wedding ring on your finger. Is that from the past, or have you managed to find a new partner too?"

"Yes, I'm married to a vet. Mark and I make a great team. He saved my cat after members of the same gang that killed my husband poisoned it."

"How dreadful. I take it they issued you a warning."

"Yes, but it didn't work. They were caught and dealt with. Mark and I started dating, and the rest is history."

He smiled. "Your eyes light up when you talk about him."

"We're very much in love. He had a recent health scare, but he's getting there."

"Glad he's on the mend. What about siblings? Do they live in Hereford?"

"I have a sister, Lesley. She flits around between jobs. At the moment, she's working in a care home. She looked after Dad after Mum died, before Margaret came into the picture. We lost our brother around five years ago. He was into drugs and overdosed one day. That was tough for the family to comprehend. I don't think my mother ever got over the shock of losing him. He was her favourite, despite her denying it for years."

"Mothers and sons have a special bond. I'm closer to my mother than my father."

"Where do your parents live?"

"Down in Devon. I grew up there. My wife, Daisy, is from Worcester. She's the one who saw the position advertised and urged me to consider it. We both love the area, the scenery et cetera. We're hoping our lads, Jack and Matt, will settle into their new schools. It's always a risk moving teenagers when they have exams ahead of them."

"I can understand that, sir."

Mary entered with the coffee, placed a cup and saucer in front of each of them, then left the room.

"Thank you, Mary," DCI Banks called after her. "She seems nice, although a little hesitant this morning."

"I suppose that is to be expected. She was very close to Price. She feels cheated, just as I do. You put all your trust in someone and... sorry, I swore I wouldn't allow that woman to get under my skin again."

"If you want to let off steam about her, now's your chance to do it."

"I don't, sir. I think it's best if we all move on and quickly. I'm not one to let things fester, not really. My motto, and with good reason, has always been that life is too short to dwell on negativity."

"I wholeheartedly agree with you. I think we're going to get on well together, Inspector."

"I hope so, sir. There's nothing worse than coming to work and walking on eggshells, wondering if your immediate boss is watching your every move, ready to pounce on any mistakes you make."

He cradled his cup in his hand and laughed raucously. "I get where you're coming from, and I want to assure you that I'm not like that at all. In my experience, a contented team always brings out the best in each individual. I have no plans to change my mindset with this role. As I said, I think we're going to get on well."

"That would be great, sir. How long have you been on the Force?"

"This will be my twenty-fifth year. Although I have to tell you, it seems like yesterday when I signed up. Where do the years go, eh?"

"Tell me about it. It's hard to believe I have already got twenty under my belt."

He took a sip from his coffee, and Sara followed suit. "They say time flies when you're having fun. Maybe that's what we've been doing all these years."

"Possibly, sir."

"Right, now we've got all the niceties out of the way, I'd like to have an open and honest discussion about what your needs are for the future."

"My needs?"

"As in, what do you and your team need in order to function properly?"

"Gosh, I haven't really thought about it. I suppose our computer equipment is getting a bit old and could do with updating."

He jotted down some notes on his pad. "Anything else?"

"You've caught me on the hop. I wasn't expecting you to ask that, sir."

"Not to worry. Can you have a think about it and get back to me sometime this week? My idea is to make changes around here, and being new to the department, I believe now is the right time to implement the changes." He winked at her. "The super will want to help me feel settled ASAP, if you get my drift?"

"I do. Thank you, sir."

"I also want you to know that my door is always open for you, whether you need to chat about an investigation or to discuss a personal issue."

"Again, thank you. It's good to know."

"You're the main reason I took this job, Sara."

She was taken aback by his words. "Sir?"

"I've done my research—maybe not on the personal side of things, but on your professional abilities—and they are second to none. You have an exemplary record at the station. Tell me, what drives you?"

"Gosh, now you're asking. I suppose I have an urge to right the wrongs in society, to be there for the victims and to seek the justice they or their families deserve after a terrible crime has been committed. My main aim is to make Hereford the best place to live, with a focus on a crime less society."

He smiled and nodded. "We're singing from the same song sheet there. Do you think it's achievable, given that crime rates have escalated since the pandemic?"

"My team and I are going to do our very best. We're not like other teams." She peered over her shoulder and lowered her voice to add, "Most of the others tend to take their time over investigations. My team is on the same wavelength as me. We set out to get to the truth of an investigation from the outset."

"Hence the reason why you have the best record at the station."

"That's not to say that we're not thorough in our research. What we do better than other teams is think outside the box. We never take an investigation at face value. You know as well as I do that criminals are getting craftier these days."

"I agree. Too many true crime programmes on TV to help guide them in committing the perfect crime."

"Yes, sadly, that's true."

"Okay. I think we've covered everything we need to here. What I'd like to add is this: please don't exclude me from your investigations. I'm not saying that you have to report to me every step of the way. Just keep me informed now and again as an interested party, not as your boss." He pointed at the pile of papers in his in-tray. "If nothing else, it'll distract me from getting bogged down with paperwork every day. That's the worst part of this job. If I can assist you out in the field anytime, don't hesitate to call me."

Sara smiled. "That's good to know, sir. I'm totally with you on the paperwork side of things, too. The bane of our lives, eh?"

"You're not wrong. Now, drink your coffee. Mary told me how much you enjoy it."

"She's right. Oh, that's another thing we can add to the list: better coffee facilities." She grinned, expecting him to see the funny side of her comment.

He jotted something down. "Too right. It's important that you have coffee that is drinkable at your disposal. Don't forget to let me know what else needs tweaking around here."

"I'll get the list back to you by the end of the week. I'll ask the team for their opinion, too."

"You do that. Well, after our open and frank discussion here today, I'm looking forward to working alongside you, Inspector Ramsey. Do you have a case on the go at the moment?"

"I'm eager to see what the future holds for us. No, we're just wrapping up the last case. It's taken us weeks because of Price's involvement. This office was torn apart by members of my team. So, you'll have to forgive us if anything is out of place, sir."

"All in a day's work, right? No gripes from me."

Sara finished her coffee and rose from her seat. "It's been lovely getting to know you, boss. Long may our relationship last, especially if we have the same objectives."

"I agree." He raised his cup. "To us, Inspector."

Sara left his office and found Mary keenly awaiting her appraisal. "He seems really nice, doesn't he?"

"I thought so as well. I was eager to hear your thoughts. It's so difficult judging someone, knowing what has gone on before."

"I think we're safe with him. I didn't pick up that he was lying to me, but who can bloody tell these days?"

"I know, it's a very awkward situation. Was he heavy-handed with you?"

"No, the complete opposite. We appear to want the same things for the area we live in. I suppose only time will tell if that's true."

"But you feel more positive about things than you did when you arrived this morning?"

"Without a doubt. Therefore, my advice to you would be to enjoy your work but keep an open mind for now." Sara touched the back of her hand. "Any doubts or suspicions on your part, you know where to find me."

"I do. Thank you, Inspector Ramsey."

"Right, I'd better get on with my working day. Call me if you need me."

"I will. Have a successful day."

Sara smiled and left the office, aware that her stomach still didn't feel right. She understood why when she entered the incident room. "Hey, what's going on?"

"I was just working up the courage to come and find you," Carla said.

"Why?"

"We've had a call about a murder. It doesn't seem good, Sara." Carla's voice was quaking.

"What murder does look good? Never mind. You can fill me in on the way." Sara collected her coat from the stand, and they set off.

"Dare I ask how it went with the chief?" Carla asked as they ran down the stairs.

"He seems friendly enough. I'm going to reserve judgement for the time being."

"Ouch. That doesn't sound too good at all."

"No, that's not what I said. He seems like a nice man. I suppose I'm bound to feel a little apprehensive, though, you know, in the circumstances."

They jumped into the car, and Sara left Carla to input the information into the satnav.

"What have we got?"

"A well-known solicitor was found murdered in his office by his secretary first thing this morning."

"Shit. Anything else?"

"Isn't that enough?" Carla shot back.

"Sorry, that's not what I meant. Is there anything else I should know? How about that?"

"Much better. The killer left a note."

"Saying what?"

"I'm not sure. That's all I was told."


They arrived at the solicitor's office a few minutes later. After parking the car, Sara collected two protective suits from her boot and handed one to Carla.

"We'll put them on closer to the scene."

At the cordon, they signed the Crime Scene Book, and a uniformed officer raised the tape to allow them to enter. Inside, they found Lorraine and her team sorting out their equipment.

"Morning, Lorraine. Are you free to talk?" Sara asked.

"Give me two ticks to get my team organised. You need to put your suits on, sooner rather than later."

"Consider us told."

Sara and Carla stepped to the side and slipped into their suits.

Sara waited for Lorraine to finish issuing orders to her team, then shouted, "Who called it in?"

Lorraine pointed at an office door. "The staff are in there. There are four of them. All shocked, as you can imagine."

"We'll get to them soon." She lowered her voice and asked, "Where's the victim?"

Lorraine thumbed towards the room behind them. "In there. I'm ready now. Come with me."

The pathologist led the way into a large office. Sitting in the chair behind a mahogany desk was the victim. His throat had been slit open, and his white shirt was now stained with blood.

"Shit," Sara muttered.

Lorraine crossed the room and stood behind the victim. "Don't ask the obvious question, will you?"

"I wouldn't dare. Any other injuries?" Sara craned her neck to look behind the victim. "He was tied to the chair before he was killed?"

"Looks that way. No other injuries. His secretary arrived at eight forty-five. She didn't check his office until nine-fifteen. She assumed her boss, Richard Manning, was running late. I think you should interview them, then release them and let them go home to recover. They're all pretty shaken up, as expected."

"Okay. Did she say how the killer got in? Was the door open when she arrived?"

"It was. She told me he was expecting a client after hours last night," Lorraine replied.

"Thanks. We'll get out of your hair. Hang on, is that the message from the killer?"

"Yep, it would seem the killer left his mark, in more ways than one."

Sara took a step forward to read the cryptic message. "'The truth is in the shadows.' How bizarre."

"Yes, not the usual type of message we've discovered at a scene in the past."

Sara removed her phone from her pocket and took a photo of the words scrawled into the desk. Then she and Carla left the room. She knocked on the office door where the staff were waiting.

Sara smiled and entered the room. "Hello, I'm sorry you've had to witness this dreadful scene today. I'm DI Sara Ramsey, the Senior Investigating Officer on the case, and this is my partner, DS Carla Jameson. Can I ask who found the body?"

A woman wiped the tears from her eyes and raised her hand. "I did. I'm Barbara. I am... sorry, I *was* Mr Manning's secretary." She sniffled, and one of the other women comforted her. "I can't believe he's gone. Who would do such a wicked thing?"

"That's what we intend to find out. The pathologist told us that Mr Manning had a late client last night. What can you tell us about that person?"

"That's right. He's Laurence Bullman. He works full-time and struggled to get here during the day, so Mr Manning agreed to stay behind to deal with him. You don't think this was down to him, do you?"

"We can't be sure. We'll need his details before we leave. Was the appointment made in person?"

"No, he rang up last week, and Mr Manning got back to him once he knew his wife would be away for the evening. Oh God, someone needs to tell her."

"Don't worry, we'll handle it. Again, we're going to need Mr Manning's address before we leave. Do you know if his wife works?"

"No. She's retired."

"Do you happen to know where she was last night?"

Barbara nodded. "Yes, she was staying at a friend's house. They were going for dinner and having a night out at the theatre."

"I see. Thank you for that information. What type of solicitor was Mr Manning? Did he specialise in any particular field?"

"No. His knowledge was vast. He refused to specialise," Barbara replied. She blew her nose on a fresh tissue. "He was such a lovely man. I can't understand why anyone would want to hurt him."

"How long has he been here?"

"Over twenty years. He owned the business."

"How many other solicitors work here?"

"Two," the lady comforting Barbara said. "Toby and I. We both joined the firm last year, a couple of months apart, because Richard was snowed under with clients."

"Thank you. Sorry, and your name is?"

"Wendy Cutler."

"Did Richard confide in either of you?"

Wendy frowned and glanced at the young man sitting opposite her.

"About what?" the man asked.

"Are you Toby?" Sara asked.

"That's correct. Confide in us about what? Are you saying you think he knew he was going to be killed?" Toby asked.

Sara waved her hand. "Not necessarily. What we need to know is if Richard has been under unnecessary stress lately. Has he had any threats from any clients he's been working with or any former clients? I know we have to chase up the man he had an appointment with last night, but if there's nothing to that meeting, then we would need to know where to look next for clues."

The four colleagues shook their heads.

"Have any of you seen anyone hanging around outside the building, acting suspiciously lately?"

Again, all the staff shook their heads.

"Do you have any cameras here?"

"Sadly not," Wendy admitted. "It was on the agenda to have them fitted in a few months. We were in the process of getting quotes from the relevant security firms."

"Thank you. We'll visit this Mr Bullman and take it from there. My advice would be for all of you to go home and allow SOCO and the pathologist to carry out their work."

"How long will that take? Will we have to give them our DNA?" Toby asked.

"Yes, if you could all provide samples of your fingerprints and DNA, that would help the investigation. These things tend to take a couple of days to complete. The SOCO team will give you an idea before you leave."

"Please do your very best to find the person responsible, Inspector," Wendy said.

"That goes without saying. We won't let you down. Can you give us the addresses of Bullman and Mr Manning now?" Sara directed her question to Barbara.

"I was told to stay in here, we all were," Barbara replied warily.

Wendy put an arm around her shoulder. "Only until we spoke to the inspector, love. She's in charge of the investigation."

On the verge of tears, Barbara sniffled. "Of course. I'm sorry, I'm not thinking straight."

"Sergeant Jameson will accompany you. That should fend off any questions from the SOCO team."

Carla nodded and smiled at Barbara. "Are you ready?"

They left the room, giving Sara the chance to have a quiet word with the others. "I'm going to need a statement from each of you in the near future. Can you give me a rough idea of what sort of man Richard Manning was?"

Wendy was the first to reply. "I think I can speak for everyone here. He was a very fair man. If he had something on his mind, he'd tell you about it. He ran an efficient office. Shared the work around equally."

"What about his home life? Was all well there?" Sara asked. She jotted down their responses.

"Yes, he often spoke about his wife and his son. He's a solicitor at another firm. There was talk about asking Nigel to join us in a couple of months. He's a property lawyer, and Richard was intending to branch out into that area."

"I see. Right, I think I have a clearer image of the man now. Again, I'm so sorry for your loss and what you've had to witness here today."

"We'll miss him," Toby said. "Personally, I've had many conversations with him about rugby. He used to play the odd game when he was at university."

"Does his son play?"

"No, he isn't interested in the sport. I think that's why Richard sometimes enjoyed spending time with me over a pint at lunchtime. Most of the time, it wasn't work-related, just an excuse to discuss the weekend games. I will miss our chats. He was very knowledgeable about the game."

Barbara and Carla returned to the room.

"All set to go?" Sara asked.

Carla nodded and waved her notebook. "Yes. We're good to go."

"Thank you for your help at this sad time. I'll arrange for uniformed officers to take down your statements soon. Carla, can you jot down everyone's phone number before we leave?"

Carla stepped towards the group, and Sara left the office. Back in reception, she surveyed the layout of the area. The front door was at the bottom of four steps. If the killer came in that way, whether it was Bullman or not, they would have had the option to open five doors off the reception area, unless Manning had kept his office door open, which was probably the likely scenario.

"What are you thinking?" Carla said behind her.

Sara slapped a hand on her chest. She turned to make sure Carla was alone, then said, "Scare the crap out of me, why don't you?"

"Sorry."

"I was just getting my bearings. It's a shame there are no cameras in the reception area, at least. Let's hope they get them fitted soon."

"It does seem unusual for a solicitor's office not to have any. They're way behind the times there."

"Maybe. It also tells us that they probably haven't felt the need to add them in the past. Perhaps their clients are the well-behaved, less fraught kind."

"Possibly. There is so much anger directed at solicitors these days. Maybe their prices are more acceptable to the general public, or am I talking bullshit after what has just happened?"

"I'll go with the latter on that." Sara grinned. "I'm going to have a quick word with Lorraine, and then we'll head over to break the news to his wife."

"Might be worth giving her a call first to see if she's returned from her night out. My guess is she hadn't up until five minutes ago; otherwise, she would have rung him, wouldn't she?"

"Not necessarily. They're an older couple. Maybe they prefer to give each other space and aren't joined at the hip. Why would she call him?"

"If she's arrived home and noticed the bed hasn't been slept in? If something doesn't feel right at home? The lack of dishes in the sink, that sort of thing."

"Possibly." Sara walked into Manning's office and stared at the man's open throat for a few seconds. She swallowed down the acid burning her mouth.

"Everything all right?" Lorraine asked.

"Yes, sorry. I was in a world of my own. Any evidence left by the killer other than the writing on the desk?"

"Nothing obvious."

"Any idea what type of knife was used?"

Lorraine glanced up and smiled. "I'm guessing one with a sharp blade."

Sara pulled a face at her friend. "You can be so obtuse at times."

"Guilty as charged. I'll let you know once the PM has been carried out. Do you want to attend?"

"Not particularly. Is there any need for me to?"

"No, but I always like to extend the invitation, just in case."

"We've got his address. We're going to head over there now to see if the wife is back home yet."

"Has she been away?"

"Overnight stay. Theatre and dinner out with a friend."

"Convenient," Lorraine said.

"We'll see. Maybe the killer found out, and that's why they chose to attack and murder the victim last night."

"That's for you to find out. I'll send over my report as soon as I can."

. . .

THEY ARRIVED at a detached house on an exclusive estate at Clehonger. There was a Mercedes parked on the drive. Sara had decided to take a punt that Mrs Manning would be home.

"Let's get this over and done with."

"I hate this part, just saying."

"You're not the only one. Just a reminder: I'm the one who has the unfortunate job of telling her."

Carla grinned before they exited the vehicle.

The garden was planted with an abundance of rose trees, which were beginning to bud, ready for the season ahead. Dotted in between were ground cover plants and a few lavender shrubs. "Looks like someone is a keen gardener. I bet the smell is beautiful in the summer."

"Whatever," Carla said, not in the least bit interested.

Sara rang the bell. A woman in her fifties opened the door wearing a dressing gown. She had a towel wrapped around her head. "Mrs Manning?"

"That's right. And you are?" Her gaze flitted between them.

Sara and Carla produced their warrant cards.

"I'm DI Sara Ramsey, and this is my partner, DS Carla Jameson. Can we come in for a chat?"

She seemed confused by the request. Her hand gripped the front of her robe. "What's this about? Have I done something wrong?"

"No, you haven't. Please, it would be better if we spoke inside."

Hesitantly, she took a step backwards and allowed them to enter the cosy hallway. "I'd prefer it if I got dressed. I feel uncomfortable talking to someone in authority wearing this. I won't be long."

She ran up the stairs before Sara had a chance to tell her not to bother. They were left waiting in the hallway for her to reappear, which turned out to be five minutes later.

"I'm so sorry. I should have told you to take a seat in the lounge." Her hair was still wet, and she'd thrown on a teal-coloured leisure suit. "Come through. Can I get you a drink?"

"No, it's fine."

They followed her into another cosy room decorated in a soft green. A wood-burning stove and ornate fireplace were the dominant features in the room.

"Take a seat. Do you mind telling me what this is about? Do I need my husband to attend this meeting? He's a solicitor based in the city."

Sara and Carla sat on the couch opposite Elizabeth Manning.

"Umm... your husband is the reason we're here," Sara said.

"He is? Why? What's he been up to?"

"It is with regret that I have to inform you that your husband passed away last night."

A hand slapped against her cheek. "No. No, this can't be right. Are you sure? I need to call him." She picked up her mobile from the coffee table and rang a number. She stared at Sara and shook her head. "There's no answer. Oh no, what do you mean he passed away? Was it his heart? Sorry, I need to call my son."

"First, can you allow me to explain what has happened?"

Elizabeth stared at Sara. "Okay, tell me." She plucked two tissues from the table and wound them around her fingers.

"Barbara, your husband's secretary, found him in his office. I'm sorry to have to tell you that Richard has been murdered."

"He what? No, I can't do this, not without my son being here."

"If that's what you want. Would you rather I call him?"

"No, I'm quite capable of speaking to my only child," she snapped. "I'm sorry, you didn't deserve to be spoken to like that. This has come as a huge shock to me."

"There's no need for you to apologise. I quite understand."

Her hand shook as she held the phone to her ear. "Sorry to trouble you, darling. Oh God, I don't know how to tell you this... I'm sorry, I can call you back after you've spoken with your client." She ended the call and broke down in tears. "He was too busy to speak with me. This can't be happening. Why would anyone want to kill my husband? He's never wronged anyone, not that I know of."

Sara went over what she knew about his late appointment the evening before. "Our next stop is to interview the man in question."

"Down at the station, I presume?"

"If it comes to it. We'll see how the land lies first."

Elizabeth's phone rang. "It's Nigel. Can I get this?"

Sara nodded. "Of course you can."

"Hello, darling. I'm so sorry for disturbing you. Thank you for getting back to me. Can you come to the house? Yes, it's urgent... Oh, I see. I suppose I'll have to tell you over the phone then. It's about your father... I have two police officers here with me... They've just told me that your father has... been murdered." She put her phone on speaker so they could all hear his reaction.

"What are you talking about, Mother? He can't be dead."

"Hello, Nigel. This is DI Sara Ramsey. I'm sorry to have to share the devastating news with you and your mother. Your father was found murdered in his office this morning."

"Murdered? How?"

"I'd rather not say at the moment, not until the cause of death has been confirmed by the pathologist."

"Jesus. Are you for real? I demand to know how he was killed."

Sara closed her eyes, dreading their reaction. "His throat was cut."

Elizabeth broke down again and sobbed. "Please, come home, Nigel."

"I'll be there shortly." He ended the call.

"I'll make you a drink," Carla offered. "Tea?"

"Yes, please. Everything is on the side in the kitchen," Elizabeth said between sobs.

Carla left the room, and Sara plucked more tissues from the box on the table. She left her seat and sat on the arm of Elizabeth's chair.

"Let it out. Hopefully, Nigel will be here soon."

"I hope so. This has come as a complete shock to me. Do you know who did it? Was it the man who requested the late appointment?"

"We're not sure. We're going to visit him next. We always inform the families first before we proceed with the investigation. I'm truly sorry for your loss."

"I didn't realise he hadn't been home. I was out with a friend last night. We had dinner and then went to a show. I spoke to him at around five-thirty yesterday. I didn't bother calling him when we got home because it was past midnight. He's an early bird, up at six every morning. He works out in the gym. I'm sorry, I'm using the wrong tense there… I can't bring myself to think of him in the past tense. He was my life. We had so many plans for our future. He was going to retire in five years, after he'd enticed Nigel to join him. It was my husband's ambition for Nigel to take over the reins from him. All our dreams have now vanished. My God, what am I going to do without him?"

Carla brought the drinks in and set them on the table in front of them. They sat in silence for the next few minutes until Elizabeth spoke again.

"Why? Why would someone go to his office with the intention of killing him?"

"We don't have any answers for you yet. We spoke to the staff at the office. They told us that Richard was a nice man and they couldn't understand why he'd been killed, either."

She shook her head repeatedly.

A voice called out from the hallway.

She gasped. "It's my son."

Nigel burst into the room. Sara left her seat, giving the pair of them room to embrace.

"What the hell happened? How was this allowed to…? Oh God, this is dreadful news. I'm so sorry, Mum. We'll get the bastard. If the police can't find the person responsible, I will spend the rest of my life hunting the fucker down."

Sara retook her seat next to Carla and raised a hand. "Please, you're going to have to give us a chance to investigate the crime first. Talking about vigilante justice isn't going to get us very far, is it?"

"It's not talk, Inspector. I'm warning you, if this person isn't arrested within the next few days, then I will do whatever it takes to find them. This person shouldn't be allowed to walk the streets, committing heinous crimes like this."

"In an ideal world, you and I know that's true. Please, my team and I won't let you down. Just give us the chance to prove ourselves."

Elizabeth gripped her son's hand. "Please don't talk like that, Nigel. We're both angry about this, but I wouldn't want to lose you as well. Why don't we leave it up to the police to find the suspect?"

"Because I know that sometimes the police don't care about the victims or their families."

Sara shook her head. "I'm sorry you feel that way, Mr Manning. My team's record tells a very different story."

"Does it? I'll be doing my own research on the matter, I can assure you."

"Which is your prerogative. At least give us a chance."

"You've got until the end of the week. After that..."

"Please finish your sentence, just so we've got a record of your intentions," Sara said.

Carla withdrew her notebook and poised her pen.

Nigel left his mother's side and paced the room. He walked over to a frame sitting on the sideboard and picked it up. He ran a finger over the photo. When he replaced it, Sara could see it was a picture of him with his parents.

"Dad wasn't the sort to invite trouble to his door. He was one of the kindest men and best solicitors I know. The amount of pro bono work he covered every month proves that."

"We'll look into that side of things as well. Thank you for telling us. I have to ask if your father has had any issues with anyone outside the office lately."

"Such as?" Nigel asked.

"Someone from the estate, if he goes to the pub or a club. Any issues there?"

Elizabeth shook her head. "We get on really well with the neighbours, and my husband doesn't belong to any clubs. We have a home gym that he used three to four times a week, rather than pay for expensive gym fees."

"What about in the past? Anything there you can think of? The reason I ask that is because we found a cryptic phrase carved into your husband's desk." Sara removed her mobile from her pocket and showed them the message.

Elizabeth and Nigel read it, then stared at each other and shook their heads.

"No, that doesn't mean anything to me. What about you, son?" Elizabeth asked.

"Nothing at all. Dad loved that desk. It was a bespoke piece that he splashed out on a few years ago. He told us he felt his office was lacking something."

"Yes, he'd never spent that much on himself before. He considered the cost of it for weeks before he finally succumbed. Now look at it; it's ruined. This person must be an animal to murder my husband and to scrawl that message into his pride and joy."

"If there's nothing else you think we should know, we're going to leave and get the investigation underway."

"There isn't, not that we can think of at this time. Maybe you can leave us both a card?" Elizabeth requested.

Sara pulled two business cards from her pocket and slid them across the coffee table. "Call me anytime, day or night. I want to assure you that we will be working diligently to find the person responsible for your husband's death."

"I should hope so," Nigel said. "If I'm not satisfied with the results, I'll come after you, Inspector."

Sara tilted her head. "Is that a threat, sir?"

"No, it's a promise. In my experience, the police are far too laid-back these days."

"In your opinion. That really isn't the case with my team. Feel free to do your research into the investigations we've solved over the past couple of years."

"I will, don't worry."

Elizabeth stood and showed them to the front door. "I'm sorry my son spoke to you that way. I shouldn't have called him."

Sara smiled. "Don't worry, we're used to people doubting our abilities after all the bad press the Force has received lately."

"It was still unnecessary. It's the anger talking. He's usually quite a placid person."

"Honestly, it's fine. You take care of yourself. I meant what I said: call me if you need anything."

"There is one thing." Elizabeth's gaze dropped to the floor.

"What's that?"

"Will I be able to say goodbye to Richard?"

"Of course you will. I'll pass on your details to the pathologist. She'll call you when it's convenient to see him. Again, I'm so sorry for your loss. Have faith in my team. We'll do our best not to let you down."

"I trust you. You've been so kind to me. Thank you."

Sara shook her hand, and they left the house. She let out a breath and groaned as they walked back to the car. "Jesus, we could have done without him showing up."

"Too right. I sense he's going to be trouble."

"Experience tells me you're right. Dealing with solicitors is never easy at the best of times. Let's see what this Bullman has to say."

## 2

—————

Sara drew up outside the address they had been given, which turned out to be a lock-up garage. "Shit! I should have known we'd be led up the garden path. I just didn't realise it was going to be this early in the investigation."

Carla slapped her hand on the dashboard. "Fuck! This is all we need, with Nigel's threat ringing in our ears."

Sara faced her and wagged her finger. "Don't even go there. How is this our fault?"

Carla sighed. "Christ, you know what this means, don't you?"

Sara frowned. "Go on."

"We've got a bloody killer intent on playing games with us."

"Bring it on. We've been here before, and none of those bastards won in the end, did they?"

"I know. However, it usually takes us a while to figure out that the shits are toying with us. It's unusual for them to make it obvious right out of the traps like this."

Sara ran a hand over her face. "Right, let's get back to the station and see what we can find out about this Laurence Bullman."

"That's a nailed-on false name."

Sara started the engine and ground her teeth all the way back to the station. She got out of the car and kicked her tyre. "I refuse to allow this to get us down. Right!"

"If you say so."

"Nope. Not on my watch, and definitely not with a new DCI to impress, either."

They entered the reception area.

"Back so soon?" Jeff, the desk sergeant, asked.

"Yes. Time to get on with the investigation. We've informed the victim's wife."

"Give me a shout if there's anything I can do, ma'am."

"Actually, you can. If you can arrange for the solicitor's office to be kept under surveillance for the next day or so, that would help. The odd drive past will do for now."

"I can do that. I'll report back with my team's findings."

"Thanks, Jeff."

They entered the security door and returned to the incident room. The team was anxious to hear the details about the investigation. Carla made them all a drink while Sara went over the crime scene with the others. "So, there we have it: a fake address for this Laurence Bullman, whose name is no doubt false as well. What we need to do is search for this man via the usual paths. Jill, can I get you to check his number for me? It'll probably turn out to be a burner phone."

"On it now, boss."

"Barry, can you try to source any CCTV footage in the area? Unfortunately, there are no cameras at the office. Would you believe they're in the process of considering getting them?"

Barry tutted and said, "It's a bit late now. I'll see what I can find."

Sara moved towards Christine, their computer expert. "I'd like you to review Manning's cases, maybe going back a couple of years. See what has been highlighted in the press, if anything. I'll get a warrant organised for the files at the office. That should cover our backs."

"Just Manning's cases, or should I go over the other solicitors' cases at the office?" Jill asked.

Sara mulled over her question and nodded. "Yes, let's do that. Might as well kill two birds and all that. Craig, why don't you and Marissa team up and go through Manning's social media accounts if he has any? Highlight anything controversial and the responses he's had from people that might give us a lead that we can follow up."

Marissa smiled and moved her chair to sit next to Craig. They put their heads together and got to work. Marissa jotted down notes while Craig pounded his keyboard and stared at his screen.

"What do you want me to do?" Carla perched on the desk next to Sara.

"I need you to do some background checks on Nigel, his son."

Carla raised an eyebrow. "Any reason?"

"Just humour me. His reaction didn't really add up for either of us, did it?"

"That's true. Okay, I'll see what I can come up with."

While the team got on with their tasks, Sara went back to her office to complete her daily chore, which had been interrupted earlier when the chief summoned her. She paused to take in the view of the Brecon Beacons that were visible on the cloudless day.

*It's too nice a day to be stuck at work. I should be out there, climbing the hills with Mark. What a day to kill someone! What a stupid thought. As if any day is a good day to commit murder!*

She chastised herself and returned to her seat.


An hour later, Sara rejoined the rest of her team, who, disappointingly, hadn't found anything worth investigating during their preliminary searches.

However, Christine raised the point that Manning had once been on a committee for council affairs, but over the years, due to the success of his business, that side of things had fallen by the wayside.

According to the team, they hadn't found any bad press about him, which left them struggling to know where to start.

"What about any cameras in the area?"

"The nearest I have found so far is from the car park opposite the solicitor's office," Craig said. "Saying that, it doesn't give me an angle that picks up the main door of the office, so I'm none the wiser. I'll keep searching for other cameras in the area."

"Okay, let's pack up for the day and, if nothing comes to light in the morning, I'll have to call a press conference and rely on the public to assist us."

The team seemed as despondent as she felt as they switched off their computers and tidied up their desks.

"Carla, can I have a quick word in my office before you leave?"

Her partner appeared surprised by the request but nonetheless followed her into her office. "Have I done something wrong?" she asked from the doorway.

Sara gestured for her to take a seat. "What makes you say that?"

"It's unusual for you to summon me at the end of the day, that's all."

"Sorry. No, I'm worried about the team. They appear pissed off, and it's only day one."

Carla flung herself into the chair. "That's because they are. I know it's only the first day, but we've usually picked up some kind of clue by now, whether through background checks or social media posts. As things stand, there's nothing to be found."

"That means we'll be reliant on finding something in the previous cases he's dealt with, so the sooner we get the warrant through, the better."

"I agree. I think you're right about calling a press conference tomorrow."

"I'll have a serious think about that this evening. I feel we need to be seen doing something positive, if only to keep Nigel off our backs."

"Again, I agree. I'm not sure what else we can do to find a suspect who doesn't want to be found."

"Barry said he still has a few cameras to check. I hope something comes from them. Right, it's been a frustrating day. Let's go home, get some rest and start over tomorrow. This evening, if you think of anything else we should be doing, let me know in the morning."

"I'll keep thinking. Enjoy your evening. Are you doing anything special?"

"Actually, Ted and Mavis, our neighbours, have invited us to dinner tonight."

"That's lovely. You haven't mentioned them lately. Are they well?"

"I think a few niggles, aches and pains are creeping in, which is hardly surprising considering they must both be in their eighties. It should be a fun evening. We always have a good time with them."

"Enjoy. See you in the morning." Carla smiled and left the office.

Sara switched off her computer and shoved the paperwork, still waiting to be addressed, back into the in-tray to deal with in the morning.


HALF AN HOUR LATER, she parked outside her house. En route, she had stopped off at the supermarket to pick up a nice bottle of wine and a cheesecake to take with them to their neighbours'.

Mark was already at home. He met her in the hallway and gave her a kiss. "How was your day?" he asked.

"Don't ask. What about yours?"

"It was passable. I only managed to get bitten once today." He laughed.

"What? Badly?"

He showed her his red hand. "No, didn't even break the skin. It was a feisty German shepherd with a painful rear end."

"Eww... I'm not surprised he bit you if you were poking around in his backside."

"I wasn't, but that's beside the point. How long are you going to be?"

"Not too long, maybe twenty minutes. Why?"

"I've fetched some paperwork home. I've got changed, ready to go. Take your time."

"And very smart you look, too." She kissed him again, made a brief fuss of Misty, her cat, then flew up the stairs to get changed. After a quick shower, she rifled through her wardrobe and finally settled on her black dress, which was smart without being too over the top. Excitement building, she applied the lightest touch of makeup and took her evening shoes from the bottom of the wardrobe.

She knew her choice was a success when her husband whistled as she entered the kitchen. Misty was sitting on his lap. He placed the cat gently on the floor and walked towards Sara.

"You should dress up more often. You look amazing." He kissed her on both cheeks and inhaled the aroma of her perfume that she'd spritzed on her neck. "That's my favourite you're wearing, too."

"What are you saying? That I look drab other times?" She laughed.

"Not in the slightest. I'm almost done here. Why don't you feed Misty while I finish off?"

"Sounds good to me. Has she been out lately?"

"Yes, not long ago."

Sara removed a sachet of food from the fridge and squeezed the contents into Misty's clean bowl. She added a few biscuits, just for a change of texture, then set the bowl on the floor. Misty pounced on her food and purred noisily while she ate.

"Looks like another satisfied customer," Mark quipped. "Maybe we should write to the company to let them know how much she enjoys their food. We might even get a year's supply as a thank you."

"Maybe a few years back, but I wouldn't hold out much hope of that happening these days. Times are tough for all of us."

"Getting tougher by the minute under the new government, but don't get me started on politics."

"I agree. I think if an election was called again, they wouldn't get in a second time. Electors never appreciate being lied to. But yes, we won't go there."

Mark completed his paperwork, and they left the house. Ted was milling by the front door and welcomed them both with a hug. The couple had been so kind to her when she'd moved in. They had instantly become good friends and now felt more like family.

"Come in. Nice to see the weather has been warmer today. Let's hope we're going to get a better summer than last year."

"The signs are good so far, Ted," Sara responded. She handed him the carrier bag containing the wine and cheesecake. "This is our contribution to the evening."

"You shouldn't have. You're always too generous."

"It works both ways. Can I help Mavis in the kitchen?" Sara asked.

"Go through and ask. I think I know what the answer will be," Ted said.

Sara left the men to it and went into the kitchen. Mavis was stirring a pot on the stove.

"Hello, lovely lady. Is there anything I can do to help?"

Mavis wiped her eyes on her apron and turned to greet Sara with open arms. "Hello, Sara. Don't mind me, I'm being silly."

Sara held her and whispered, "If you ever need to talk, I'm always here for you."

Mavis pecked her on the cheek. "You're far too busy to listen to an old crony like me wittering on."

"Not at all. If something is troubling you, then feel free to call me anytime. I regard you and Ted as my family, you know that."

"You're so sweet, Sara. I shall miss you."

Sara frowned. "What? Are you two leaving?" she asked, shocked.

Mavis' eyes watered with fresh tears. "I had no intention of spoiling your evening with us..." She paused and took a gulp. "I went to the doctor's a couple of weeks ago and again yesterday to receive the results."

Sara turned down the gas on the cooker, guided Mavis to the table and forced her to sit. "What results?"

Mavis inhaled a large breath and closed her eyes. "I have lung cancer. I've been told it's terminal. There's nothing they can do for me."

"What? Oh no, that's dreadful news. How can they tell you they can't do anything for you? How long have you been ill?"

"Months. I put off going to see the doctor because I was too scared to hear what he'd have to say. Now... I've left it too late for them to treat me."

"My goodness, at least they can try. You should get a second opinion."

"That's what Ted said. We're booked in to see another doctor privately, tomorrow. I can't complain. I've had eighty-two years on this earth, and it'll be nice to be reunited with Susie after all these years."

Sara held her hand as tears welled up. "Don't talk like that. At least wait until you get the second opinion." It was then that she noticed how frail and gaunt Mavis had become since they'd last met for dinner.

The couple had lost their daughter, Susie, decades ago, when she was only twenty-two. She'd been killed in Australia while on a back-packing holiday. The suspect was never caught. That's why Sara meant so much to them. Ted and Mavis regarded her as their replacement daughter. They'd hit it off straight away when they all moved into the new estate within months of each other.

Sara hugged Mavis. "Please, promise me you won't give up."

"I can't promise that, love. I haven't felt like myself in months. I think I'm resigned to going now. My thoughts are with Ted and, of course, what will happen to him and Muffin when I eventually go."

Muffin whimpered. He was sitting under the table, and Sara hadn't even noticed the poodle there. She slid her hand down to ruffle his head.

"You know as well as I do that Mark and I will always be here for all of you. Please don't think about that for now. Your priority has to be getting a second opinion, and quickly. We'll deal with the consequences together when the time comes."

"What would we do without you, Sara? No one could ever replace our daughter, but since we met you, you've come a very close second. It was fate, all of us moving to this estate around the same time. It must have been."

"I believe that to be true. Hey, you've always been there for me in the past. We're family, please don't ever forget that. Now, dry your eyes and let's push aside our problems for one evening. What do you say?"

"You're right. Thank you for being you."

"Nonsense. What can I do to help?"

"You can lay the table in the dining room for me, if you wouldn't mind. I asked Ted to do it, but I think he got waylaid with a faulty bulb that needed changing."

"Leave it with me. Are you sure you want to go ahead with this evening?"

"Absolutely. Sorry I've put a downer on it."

"You haven't." Sara pulled Mavis to her feet and gave her a big hug. "Remember, Mark and I are always here for you and Ted. We'll drop everything to help out, you know that."

"Thank you. We'd be lost without you."

"Likewise. Now, pin that smile in place, and let's enjoy our evening. Set aside what might be, and we'll worry about that tomorrow. Deal?"

"That's a deal. Thank you, Sara. You truly are one in a million."

Sara hugged her again and left the kitchen. She wandered through to the dining room to find the table already laid. She made a few tweaks, adding the female touch here and there, and then joined Mark and Ted in the lounge.

Ted was putting on a brave face, she could see that now. She hugged him, and he went into the kitchen to fetch them both a drink.

"How's Mavis coping? Does she need a hand in the kitchen?" Mark asked.

"No, she's fine. The table is all laid. How was Ted?"

"Ted's the same as he always is, full of zest and vigour. I'm not sure where he gets his energy from. I doubt if I'll have that much at his age."

"They're both fabulous for their age."

He hooked an arm around her shoulder. "We're lucky to have them as friends."

"We are."

"Right, enough of that, you two," Ted said as he handed them both a glass of wine. "Mavis wants us all to make our way into the dining room."

"I feel guilty not lending her a hand," Sara said.

"She's fine. She wants you two settled first, and then we'll ferry the plates out between us."

Sara and Mark linked hands and entered the dining room. They sat in their usual spots, and Ted and Mavis brought in the meals.

The evening went well. Sara and Mavis shared a few secret glances and winks during the meal. Ted made a toast to honour their friendship with a knowing tear in his eye. Mark seemed to be the only one oblivious to what was going on.

The wine and the cheesecake accompanied the beef casserole that Mavis had been slaving over all day. The food was appreciated by everyone. Sara was glad to see Mavis' appetite hadn't been hampered by the news of her illness.

The hugs as they left were stronger and more heartfelt. "Let me know what the doctor says when you see him. We love you," Sara whispered in Mavis' ear.

"I will. We love you, too, Sara," Mavis whispered back before they parted.

The couple waved until Sara and Mark reached their front door. Sara blew them both a kiss.

"Is there something going on that I don't know about?" Mark asked after they'd removed their shoes and relocated to the lounge.

She gathered his hands in hers and sighed heavily. "When I went to say hello to Mavis, I found her in tears."

Mark twisted in his seat to face her. "Oh no. Is there something wrong?"

"Mavis has been diagnosed with lung cancer."

Mark gasped and shook his head. "How awful. Is there anything they can do for her?"

"The doctor said she's left it too late for them to do anything."

"Shoot! That's not good news. What about a second opinion?"

"They're seeking it tomorrow; they've had to go private. I feel so sorry for her. I've told her to get in touch if they need anything."

"Oh my. I'm shocked and appalled to hear this. I know how much they both mean to you. I think the absolute world of them, too. Bloody cancer. It sucks!"

She leaned forward to kiss him. "I know, it's affected us all. It's time they found a bloody cure for it."

"I'll second that."

They shared a silent cuddle for the next ten minutes, both lost deep in thought. Then Sara let Misty out, and they retired to bed.

# 3

He watched and waited for the car to leave the school premises, then followed Alan Fletcher out of the gates, keeping a fair distance behind him. At the roundabout, he made sure two cars got between them, then took up the chase once more, aware of what direction Alan would be taking if he was going home.

They drove out into the countryside. By now, the other two cars had taken a different route. He dropped back a few feet. Alan indicated right, taking the lane that would eventually lead to his house. They hadn't gone far when the car stopped. He got close to it as Alan got out to inspect it. The road was too narrow to let anyone pass. Alan noticed him and approached his car. He lowered the window to chat to him.

"Sorry, mate. I think you're going to have to reverse back to the main road. Mine has just conked out on me."

"Sorry to hear that. I enjoy tinkering with cars; I can have a look for you."

Fletcher's eyes lit up. "That would be great, if you have the time."

"No problem. I'm not in a rush to get home."

"I really appreciate it."

He got the car started within a few minutes, and they both jumped back into their respective vehicles and continued their journey.

"There's one born every minute," he muttered.

Fletcher drove another five minutes before the car died on him again. This time, the road was wider. A forest ran alongside them. Fletcher flew out of his car, but this time he ignored him and drove straight past. It was all part of his plan. He watched Fletcher's reaction in his rearview mirror and grinned.

"Don't worry. I'll be back."

He drove another five hundred yards then parked in the lay-by close to the forest. He took his bag of goodies with him and, under cover of the trees, worked his way back to where Fletcher had broken down. As he got closer to Fletcher's car, he crouched lower, careful where he trod in case he alerted his target to his whereabouts. His heart rate increased rapidly, tipping the scales.

Fletcher was talking on his mobile. No, he was shouting at a loved one, telling them how stupid they were for not being able to get him out of the fix he was in. When Fletcher hung up, he made his move. He removed the bow and arrow from his bag and took aim.

*Five, four, three, two, fire!*

The arrow pierced Fletcher's leg. He yelled out and stared at the quiver sticking out of his thigh. Then he frantically glanced around him.

The bowman took aim with a second arrow and fired. This time, Fletcher stepped to the side, and the arrow landed on the road two feet to his left. "What the fuck! Who's there? What do you want?"

It was time for the game to begin. The bowman stepped out of the shadow of the tree and walked to the edge of the road, his bag by his side. "Surprise. I bet you never thought you'd see me again, did you?"

Fletcher cried out, the pain from his leg overwhelming him. "What kind of sick shit are you? First, you help me, and the next minute, you're taking shots at me. Why?"

The bowman placed a finger on his chin. "Let me think about that for a moment or two. Ah yes, because the ball is in my court. Don't worry, you deserve what's coming your way."

"How? I don't know you. If you have a problem with me, let's discuss it like adults."

"I don't have a problem with you per se, but I do detest you and what you stand for."

Fletcher narrowed his eyes. "What I stand for? You're talking about my sexuality? You despise the fact that I'm gay and married to a man?"

"Nope. Guess again. Oops... time's up. We need to get on with the game now. See how bored I get? Let's see if we can rectify that, shall we?"

Shaking his head, Fletcher looked around him. "What are you talking about?"

He dropped his bag and aimed his bow and arrow at Fletcher's head. "Get running."

"What? I can't. My leg hurts. I'm injured. I won't be able to get far."

The bowman shrugged. "That's up to you. Now, if you value your life, you'll get moving." He raised the bow.

"No, please. Don't do this."

"Move!"

Fletcher started running as fast as he could on one healthy leg, dragging the other. He fired another couple of arrows, one to the right and the other to Fletcher's left, as his target disappeared into the forest. The chase gained momentum when Fletcher upped his pace, probably sensing he might be able to outrun his attacker.

The bowman's plan had worked. It was always a clever ploy to let the target believe they had a chance of getting away in a game of this nature. He laughed and aimed another arrow. This time, the arrow struck Fletcher's good leg. He stopped running, took aim and fired yet another one.

Fletcher dropped to the ground, clutching his leg. It didn't take long to reach him.

"You should have been faster on your feet. Now look at you."

"Please, please, what do you want from me?" Fletcher screeched.

"Nothing. I'm on course to end your life. That's all you need to know." The bowman scanned the area, searching for a suitable tree, then dipped his hand into his bag. He removed a length of rope and tugged at Fletcher's collar, forcing him to his feet. "Move it."

"I can't move. Both my legs are injured now, in case you haven't noticed."

"Are you sure you're not just trying my patience?"

"No. Look at me! Jesus. I can't move now."

The bowman glanced around him at the trees close at hand and chose the nearest one. He dragged Fletcher by the hair and pinned him to the tree with one hand while he threw the rope around the trunk. He caught the other end and wrapped it several times around Fletcher's torso, securing it tightly.

"What the fuck are you doing?" Fletcher asked.

"I thought you were an intelligent man. Aren't teachers supposed to have a higher IQ than the ordinary man on the street? That's what my teacher used to tell me." He gasped. "Don't tell me he was lying to me!"

Fletcher grunted. "I know what you're doing. That much is obvious. What I meant was, *why* are you doing this to me? I don't know you, do I?"

"Nope. Ah-ha, that's going to keep you guessing until you're rescued. If anyone finds you out here." The bowman let out his most sinister laugh.

"You're going to leave me here?" There was a note of relief to his tone.

"Yes, with the caveat that I will return, or I might, depending on how I feel later."

Fletcher wriggled to try to get out of his restraints. "You can't leave me here. It's going to be dark soon."

The bowman pulled back his sleeve and glanced at the time on his gold watch. "Now, now, not for a few hours yet. Don't worry, I'm going to call at your house now and keep hubby entertained so he doesn't miss you."

"What do you mean by that? He knows I've broken down. He'll probably be on his way out here now to find me."

"Who are you trying to kid? What type of fool do you take me for?" He removed a knife from the bag along with a thin lipstick and a piece of paper. The bowman wrote, 'The past cannot be erased', ensuring that Fletcher saw the words he'd written.

"What does that mean?"

"Time will tell." Then he raised the knife and plunged it several times into Fletcher's legs before delivering another jab to his chest. Fletcher screamed. He withdrew an old sock from his bag and shoved it into Fletcher's mouth. "You're a fool if you think you can outwit me. For that, I'm going to leave you here to rot. There are wild boars in this forest. Once they get a whiff of your blood, they'll come along and tear you to shreds before someone can find you."

Fletcher cried and shook his head as tears dripped onto his cheeks. He was powerless to do anything except stare at his attacker.

The bowman removed something from the lining of his bag. It was a needle. He attached the note to the man's jacket, avoiding his wounds. He wanted whoever found him to give the note to the police. Then, he patted Fletcher on the head and walked away. "Any last messages for hubby?"

Fletcher's response was muffled by the sock.

The bowman returned to his car as a calmness descended.

*No one is likely to find him out here, not anytime soon, anyway. Two down, more to come!*

# 4

Sara and Carla were passing through the reception area on their way out of the station when something caught Sara's attention. Ears pricked, she walked over to Jeff, who was taking a call.

"Please, calm down. Can you start from the beginning for me?"

"Put it on speaker," Sara mouthed to him.

He pressed the button, and the three of them listened as the distraught man told them that he'd received a call from his husband to say that he'd broken down. When he arrived at the scene about thirty minutes later, the car was there but his husband was missing.

"Have you checked the area?" Jeff asked.

"The immediate area, yes. But there's a forest right beside the road. I'm worried he might have injured himself and wandered off. Please, can you send someone out here to help me?"

Sara glanced at Carla. "Are you up for it?"

"Really? At this time of night?" Carla grumbled.

Sara grinned and faced Jeff again. "We'll attend, along with a patrol car, just in case they're needed. Get the directions for us."

"Hello, sir, yes, I'll send someone out to assist you now. Can you give me your exact location?"

Sara and Carla stepped away from the desk, and Jeff took the phone off speaker.

"Why are you so interested in this?" Carla asked.

"You know what it's like when you get a feeling in your gut about something."

"Yeah, that feeling is hunger pangs for me. I was looking forward to stopping off at the chippy on the way home. That ain't going to happen now, thanks to your willingness to get involved."

"Misery guts. It'll probably be something and nothing, but I feel the need to check it out. Let's just say I'd rather take a shufti now than get home and be called out later to attend a scene."

"How do you do that?"

Sara frowned. "What?"

"Always manage to say the right thing to make me feel guilty and get me to change my mind."

Sara grinned and punched her partner playfully in the arm. "Good girl. The sooner we get out there, the sooner you can get home to enjoy your fish and chips. Actually, that's not a bad shout. I might call Mark on the way to see if he fancies the same for our dinner."

"Glad to be of service."

Sara collected the address from Jeff, and they drove both cars out to East Bishop. They found the man who had reported his husband missing sitting in the car with the door open.

"Thank God you're here. I just know something's wrong. I mean, why would he leave the car? He wouldn't. I know Alan. He would have stayed with the vehicle. Either someone has taken him, or he's wandered off somewhere." He shook his head. "But I know deep down that he would have stayed with his vehicle. It was unlocked when I got here, with the keys in the ignition. That alone makes me suspicious."

"It's okay. If Alan is out here, we'll find him. The patrol car should be here soon; they were right behind us. We'll conduct a search of the area. Have you tried calling him?"

He picked up a mobile from the centre console. "His phone is here. Again, it's a red flag to me. He keeps it close at all times."

"Okay, try to remain calm. We'll have a quick look around and see what we can find. Prior to today, was he having problems with the car?"

"No, it was serviced a couple of weeks ago. If anything, he said she was running like a dream. That's why none of this is making any sense. Please, please, you have to help me find him. I can sense that something is wrong. We get that sometimes, picking up when something isn't quite right with the other. It's like we've got a sixth sense about things."

"Try not to worry. Hopefully, we'll get to the bottom of things soon. Ah, here are the other officers now."

The patrol car came to a stop behind Carla's. Two male officers strode towards them. Sara met them and explained the situation. Then, the four of them headed into the woods, leaving Joe Fletcher sitting in his husband's car in case he returned.

Sara and Carla walked several feet up the road until Sara spotted a patch of blood.

"Don't make a big thing of this. Joe is watching us."

"Shit, it looks fresh." Carla's gaze travelled to the forest. "Do you think he's in there, injured?"

"Seems likely to me. Let's take a quick look. There's still enough light left. If we can't find him, then we're going to have to call for backup and conduct a thorough search, which could take a while to organise. We'll worry about that later. Come on."

They entered the forest and picked their way through the damp undergrowth. The area had seen a lot of rain over the past few weeks. It was April, after all.

"Alan, can you hear me?" Sara shouted.

She paused to listen in case the man called out for help. Nothing. So, they continued on their quest through the trees. The further they went, the denser the forest became.

"Do you really think we're going to find him?"

"We won't know unless we try." Sara's phone rang. She'd given her number to the other officers so they could contact her if they found anything. "DI Ramsey."

"Hello, ma'am. We've found him."

"Great. Is he alive?"

"Barely. You're going to need to see this."

"Where are you?"

"I'll drop a pin for our location."

Sara paused and then opened the notification she received. "I've got it. We're not far. See you soon." She quickened her pace and wove through the trees to the east, with Carla right behind her.

Up ahead, she saw one officer standing and the other crouching next to the victim. "What the fuck? He's tied to a bloody tree."

"Christ. This doesn't look good. If he's bleeding, we're going to need an ambulance out here ASAP," Carla said.

They arrived to find the man clinging to life. Sara could already see that he had several injuries to his chest and legs.

"Have you called for an ambulance?"

"Not yet. I'll do it now," the officer standing replied. He took a few steps away from them to make the call.

Sara crouched beside the victim and took his pulse. It was dangerously weak. She didn't want to believe it, but she had a hunch the man wouldn't last long. "We need to stem the bleeding. Let's put some gloves on. Have you got any blankets in the car?"

"We've got some foil blankets, and I've got a few towels. I'll fetch them."

"Quickly. Don't get into a conversation with the husband. We need those items fast."

The officer sprinted through the trees back to the road.

Sara was unsure what to do next. Her first thought was to save the man, but that was swiftly followed by her need to preserve the crime scene. She read the note pinned to the man's chest and shook her head.

Carla moved to stand behind her. "What are you thinking? That the cases are connected?"

"Seems that way, but why leave him out here to die?"

"Unless Alan fooled him into thinking he was already dead before the killer left the scene."

Sara nodded. "It seems too rushed. Maybe the killer was aware that Alan had called his husband and that he might show up to help him." She shook Alan's arm. "Alan, can you hear me?"

Alan groaned, and his eyes flickered open. "Please, help me..." he whispered, his voice trailing off.

A noise sounded behind them. The other officer had returned, carrying the foil blanket. Carla took it from him and handed it to Sara.

"Stay with us, Alan. The ambulance is on the way," Sara said.

"No! Alan..."

Sara glanced over her shoulder to see Joe running towards them.

Carla stood in his path, but he swept her aside. She slammed into a tree, the impact knocking the wind out of her. The officer who had fetched the blanket restrained Joe, preventing him from getting closer.

"Sorry, Joe. We need to preserve the scene for any evidence that might be here," Carla said.

"I don't give a flying fuck about that. He needs help."

"We've called for an ambulance. Why don't you get on the other side and talk to him?" With her gloves on, Sara removed the note.

Carla held out an evidence bag, and she slotted the note inside. Then, Sara covered Alan with the blanket, sensing that Lorraine would probably reprimand her if she were called to the scene. Right now, she felt it was important to keep Alan alive; they'd worry about the evidence side of things later. "Alan, can you hear me?"

His eyes fluttered, but there was no response.

"He's not going to die, is he?" Joe asked, on the verge of tears.

"Keep talking to him. We need to keep him awake."

"Alan. Please, stay with us. I don't want to lose you," Joe pleaded, fresh tears running down his cheeks.

"He... help... he... help me," Alan stuttered before he took his final breath.

*Shit, shit, shit!* Sara was forced to react quickly. She got to her feet and tugged at Joe to stand. "Come on, Joe. It's too late. He was too far gone for us to save him."

Joe turned on her, anger blazing in his eyes. "No, you can't say that. It's not too late. You can try to save him. I know CPR. I can do that. You can't give up on him. You just can't."

She swallowed down the lump in her throat. "I'm sorry, he's lost too much blood. Even if we brought him back to life, we wouldn't be able to do anything for him without specialised equipment to keep him alive."

"No... don't tell me that. You have to try. He's all I've got. We love each other."

Sara held out her arms and hugged him. "I'm sorry, truly I am." Tears blurred her vision, and she looked around her at the others. In the distance, she could hear a siren wailing.

Joe pulled out of her arms. "They're here. Please, you have to try to save him."

Sara sighed heavily. "I'm sorry. He's gone. He's lost too much blood. There's nothing anyone can do for him now."

Joe attempted to get to his husband, but the uniformed officers realised what his intentions were and blocked his path. He sobbed and sank to his knees.

Sara shook her head, her heart going out to the man. He shouldn't have been here to witness this atrocity. It was something that should never have happened.

*Two murders within hours of each other. What the fuck is going on here?*

Carla tapped her on the shoulder. "Are you all right?"

Sara wiped away her tears and removed a tissue from her pocket. She blew her nose and stared at Joe, who was also breaking his heart just a few feet away from his husband. "We need to call Lorraine."

"Do you want me to do it?"

"No, I'll do it. Watch him. Don't let him get any closer to Alan," she whispered, giving the order. She walked out of the forest and onto the road to make the call. "Lorraine, it's me. Sorry to call you so late. I'm at a crime scene, out near Eaton Bishop. The victim was alive when we got here, but he's since passed away. I think the case we attended yesterday is linked to this one. I found a note attached to his body."

"Shit. Okay, I was about to go home. I guess my plans for the evening have now changed. I'll be there within fifteen minutes. Hang tight until I get there and don't go near the body."

"We won't. His husband is here. We'll take him back to the car."

"Good. Do what you need to do to preserve the scene."

"See you soon." Sara ended the call.

She glanced down the road as the wail of the siren grew louder. The ambulance came around the corner, and Sara waved her arms to get their attention. The driver flashed his lights to acknowledge her. She stamped her feet to remove the mud from her boots while she waited. The vehicle drew to a halt in front of her, and two paramedics jumped out, ready for action.

"I'm sorry, you've had a wasted trip; the man has passed away."

"Heck. We should still take a look at him, just in case."

"Please do. I've been in touch with the pathologist; she's on her way. She's asked me to preserve the crime scene. He was murdered."

"Sorry to hear that," the male paramedic said.

He removed his bag from the back of the ambulance, and they both followed Sara to the crime scene.

Carla had her arm around Joe, consoling him. As soon as he saw the paramedics, he shrugged her arm off and ran towards them.

"Please, you have to help him. They're prepared to let him go. He's not been gone long. The least you can do is try to bring him back."

"Step back please, sir. We'll assess him and see if there's anything we can do to help."

The officers formed a wall, preventing Joe from seeing what was going on with his husband.

"Get out of my way. I have a right to be here. I need to see what they're up to."

"Actually, you don't have a right to be here," Sara corrected him. "This is a crime scene. Please remember that, Joe."

He turned his back on them all and ran over to a nearby tree. He put his forearm on the trunk, rested his head against it and sobbed.

Keeping one eye on him and the other on the paramedics, Sara stepped closer to the victim. "It's pointless trying, isn't it?"

The male checked Alan's heart with a stethoscope and nodded. "Yes. It's too late for him now. If you've already called the pathologist, there's nothing else we can do here. The victim has lost too much blood."

"I concur. Thanks for coming."

"It's our job. Sorry we didn't get the chance to try to bring him back. It was too late when we got here."

"It was," Sara agreed.

The paramedics left the area.

Joe tried to stop them from leaving. "No, come back. You haven't even tried to save him. I'm going to put in a complaint against all of you. You should have at least tried…"

Sara approached him. "I'm sorry. It was just too late. Are you up to giving us a few details or would you prefer to leave it until the morning?"

"No. Ask your damn questions."

"Why don't we go back to the cars?" Sara suggested.

"Here's fine. I want to be with him."

Sara removed her notebook from her pocket. "Where did Alan work?"

"He was a primary school teacher at Ashworth School. He was on his way home."

"On his way home when he rang you to say his car was having problems?"

"Yes, that's right. His car had come to a standstill on the road out there. I tried it, but it wouldn't start. I came as quickly as I could. I'd just had a shower after my session at the gym… If only I had got here sooner, he would probably still be alive."

"There's no guarantee; you mustn't blame yourself, Joe."

"Easy for you to say. I'm going to report you. You should have done more to save him. You didn't."

"I'm sorry you believe that. I'll give you my card and the name of my senior officer. It's your prerogative to report the incident. I'll have to give my account, obviously. The paramedics have confirmed that Alan had lost a lot of blood. It would have been nigh on impossible to save him."

"But you could have tried. You didn't. I find that shocking behaviour, and you need to be pulled over the coals for it."

"We'll see. I'm sorry you feel I've let you down. I can assure you, I only had your best interests at heart. I have to ask, has Alan had any issues with anyone lately?"

"No, nothing. Just because we're gay, it doesn't mean that people are out to get us all the time. Not in our experience. What about that note? I didn't get to read it properly. What did it say?"

"*The past cannot be erased.* Do you have any idea what that might mean?"

"None whatsoever. What about you? You're supposed to be the detective."

"We'll do some digging and try to find out. What about at the school? Any issues with the other teachers, or perhaps a bad experience with one of the parents?"

"No, nothing that I know about, anyway. My husband was a good man. He always put other people before himself. I don't know why anyone would want to kill him. It's unthinkable, in fact."

"Okay, thank you, that's all I need to know for now. Can I take down your number and your address?"

"Why?"

"It's procedure. Do you need a lift back home?"

"No, I'll be fine. Do I have to leave now? Is that what you're trying to tell me?"

"Yes. The pathologist will need to have access to the area. The fewer people around, the easier her job will be."

He slammed his fists against his thighs and strained his neck to peer over her shoulder. "What will happen to him?"

"A post-mortem will be carried out, either today or tomorrow."

"Do you have to? What's that going to do to his spirit?" Joe wept and covered his face with his hands.

Sara rolled her eyes at Carla. "I'm sorry, it's procedure. The pathologist will explain to you what happens to the body once the person stops breathing."

Carla shook her head and mouthed, "Lorraine is going to crucify you."

She shrugged. "We should accompany you home, Joe, to make sure you get there in one piece."

"I'm okay. I need to visit a friend. I won't be able to go home straight away. We've not long moved in. It was our first home together. I can't bear the thought of going home alone... without him."

"If that's what you'd prefer. We'll need to take a statement from you in the next couple of days. There's no rush."

"Is that how the investigation is going to be for you? Laid-back?"

"Who said that?" Sara queried. "All I'm saying is that we'll need a statement from you *when* you're ready to give us one."

"Sorry. I'm not usually this aggressive with people."

Sara rubbed his upper arm. "Don't worry, it's understandable in the circumstances. I want to assure you that we'll do our very best to find the person responsible for killing Alan."

"I hope so. This sort of thing is happening all too often in today's society. Someone needs to stamp it out. The prisons are overcrowded and offenders are being released early. What sort of message is that sending out to the criminals?"

Sara raised her hand and nodded. "Hey, I totally agree with you. Unfortunately, no one from the government bothered to ask our opinion on the idea before they went ahead and put it into action."

"It doesn't bode well for our future, does it? How many more victims have to die horrendous deaths like this before the government sits up and takes notice?"

"I'd like to know the answer to that one myself." She slipped her hand into her jacket pocket and removed a card. "Please ring me if you need to ask any questions or think of anything that might assist us in our investigation."

"Thank you. You'd better take down my details."

She jotted down his number and address and tucked her notebook back in her pocket again. "I'll pass your number to the patholo-gist. She'll be in touch within the next twenty-four hours. Don't worry; she'll take care of him."

He peered over his shoulder at his husband, who was now covered by the blanket. "I hope so. What a way to go, and at his age, too. Who could have predicted this is how his life would end? Mine, too, without him."

"I'm so sorry. It shouldn't have ended this way, that much is clear. Take care of yourself."

"Thank you." His shoulders slumped as he walked back to his car.

"I feel for him," Carla said. "What do you want to do now?"

"We'll wait for Lorraine and her team to arrive then leave them to it. They might be at it for hours out here. We'll begin the investigation in earnest in the morning."

They returned to the crime scene and instructed the two officers to set up a cordon at the entrance to the forest. Sara stood around ten feet from the victim and tapped a finger against her cheek. "Why is the killer intent on leaving us notes?"

"I was wondering the same. Hey, here's something else I've thought about."

Sara faced Carla and tilted her head. "Go on, you know I'm always open to suggestions."

"Well, do you think we might be dealing with a female killer here? You know, it's not every day we find a note written in lipstick at a crime scene."

Sara raised her eyebrows. "Good thinking. You're right, it's not. It's definitely something we need to bear in mind. There's something else that is bugging me: the fact that both crimes lacked any camera surveillance."

"Telling us they were premeditated, and the victims weren't just killed randomly."

Sara nodded. "Yep. Let's hope the killer has done the necessary now and we don't have any other murders to contend with in the near future."

It was another ten minutes before Lorraine and her team arrived.

Sara met them at the roadside and apprised them of the situation. "He died soon after we found him. The paramedics showed up not long after, but we could tell by the amount of blood he'd lost it would be pointless trying to revive him."

Lorraine nodded. "Okay, thanks for the update. There's no need for you to hang around. I'll call you later if we find anything significant."

Sara dug out the note from her pocket. Lorraine read it through the evidence bag. "Written in lipstick, eh? That's got to be a first. Have you taken a photo of it? I'll hand it to the lab when I return and get the techs working on it ASAP."

Sara removed her phone from her pocket, snapped off a few photos and handed the note back to Lorraine. "All done. I don't mind hanging around for a while if you want me to."

"No. You'll only get in the way." Lorraine grinned.

"Before you go, we found a patch of blood on the road. That's what led us to check the forest." She pointed ahead of her at the location.

"We'll take a sample to see if it belongs to the victim or the killer. Goodnight, ladies."

"In other words, bugger off." Sara laughed. "We can take a hint. Speak later or tomorrow."

"You can count on it." Lorraine picked up her bag and entered the forest. She fired off instructions to a member of her team to assess the spot of blood.

Sara and Carla parted at their vehicles.

"I'll see you in the morning," Sara said. "I'll be in early if you fancy joining me."

Carla tutted. "I'll be there. Enjoy what's left of your evening."

"I'll try. You too." Before she drove off, Sara rang Mark. "Hi, I'm heading home now. Are you still at work?"

"Good timing. I'm just packing up to leave. I thought about stopping off at the chip shop on my way home."

Sara laughed. "Great minds. I'll do it. What do you fancy?"

"The usual, haddock and chips. Can you stretch to a curry sauce on the side?"

"I'm sure I can. I'll see you soon." She ended the call and rang the local chip shop to place the order, saving some time.

During the drive, she mulled over the two crimes. The similarities regarding the notes and the inconvenience of not having any cameras around was something they would need to focus on in the morning. The victim was obviously followed out to the forest. Joe had told her that his house wasn't far. Did that mean that Alan took the route regularly? Yet another angle they should consider.

*Joe also mentioned that Alan had called him to tell him that his car had broken down. Did that mean the killer had sabotaged his vehicle in some way?*

She rang Lorraine while the thought was fresh in her mind.

"Yes! I thought we agreed that I would call you later."

"We did. I've just remembered something that your team should check out while they're there."

"What's that?"

"The victim rang his husband to say that his car had broken down. It only went in for a service recently, so that struck me as odd. Maybe the killer tampered with it."

"All right. We'll arrange to get the vehicle collected and assess it back at the lab. Can I get on now, please?"

"Yes, sorry. As you were. Good luck."

"I wouldn't need it if a certain detective inspector didn't feel the need to ring me every ten minutes."

"Hey, that's not fair. It was one call and..." She stopped when she realised Lorraine had hung up on her. "You'll keep. I'll get you back for that, matey."

SHE ARRIVED home thirty minutes later.

Mark joined her in the hallway and relieved her of her package. "I've laid the table. How was your day? Or shouldn't I ask?"

"We'll talk about it later. Right now, I'm starving and eager to eat my dinner. What about you? Did you have a good day?"

"Ditto, we'll have a natter later."

In the kitchen, Misty wound herself around Sara's legs. She picked up her cat and kissed her. "I've missed you today, munchkin. Have you been a good girl?"

"As far as I can tell," Mark replied. "Her tray will need cleaning after dinner, though."

"Don't worry, I'll do it."

Mark plated up the takeaway and, as it was later than normal, they decided to be slobs for the evening and took it through to the lounge to eat while they watched TV.

Sara flicked on the TV, pleased that news of the murders hadn't broken yet. That would all change tomorrow. She sensed they were going to need to call a press conference to get the ball rolling on both investigations.

"You're miles away. Anything you want to share?" Mark said. He finished his last mouthful and put his plate on the floor beside him. "Hold that thought. There's some wine open in the fridge. Fancy a glass?"

"I need to keep a clear head; you have it. I'll have an orange juice, please."

"Is there a chance you might get called out this evening?"

She looked up at him and shrugged. "I don't think so, but there's always a possibility."

He tutted and left the lounge. Sara switched the TV to the other news station to see if they were running either of her cases. They weren't.

Mark came back and handed Sara her drink. "You've turned over. We don't have to watch the news again, do we?"

"No. I was interested, that's all. I can switch it off."

He sat beside her, and they held hands.

"So, why were you miles away? What's going on in that pretty little head of yours?"

"Another murder came our way today. That's why I was late. We received the call as we were leaving, informing us that a man had gone missing. Carla and I drove out to the scene to find the man still alive, but he was fading fast. It was awful. Not something that we've encountered before over the years. His husband was at the scene."

"Ouch. I bet that heightened the tension for you and Carla."

"It did. The thing is, we now believe both cases are linked."

"Why would you think that?"

"The victim had a note pinned to his chest."

"Ah, okay. What did the note say?"

Sara withdrew her phone and read out the message.

"Damn. Do you have any clues yet?"

"Nope. I can see us chasing our tails for a while on this one. The killer is leaving us these notes for a reason. What that is, at this stage, is completely unknown to us."

"Do you think they're going to kill again?"

"Who knows? They might have already achieved their aim. There again, this might just be the beginning of a lengthy killing spree."

"God, I hope you're joking. I know we're just chatting, but if you said that when you're out in the field, it might cause a riot. Hereford isn't as safe as it used to be."

Sara sighed and rested her head back against the cushion. "Tell me about it. The crime rate has escalated since I took up my position here."

"Purely coincidental. A lot has happened since then, darling. The dreaded pandemic for a start."

Sara snorted. "At least that saw a dip in the crime rates. It seemed to soar after lockdown was over, though."

"People were frustrated with the government, those useless sods. Nope, I'm not going there... Partygate comes to mind."

"This country has a new leader, one they voted in, and look at what we're having to deal with now... no, I refuse to go there. Someone needs to get on top of the crime rates in this country. It's out of our hands if they keep making cutbacks. That's clearly not the answer. We need to go back to having bobbies on the streets, but that's never going to happen, not in my lifetime."

"Sorry you have to deal with this shit. What about changing your career?"

She turned to face him. "Are you kidding me? I couldn't do that. I wouldn't know where to begin for a start. Hey, ignore me. I haven't had a whinge in a while. You'll have to forgive me. Damn, I need to check in on Mavis. She was going for her second opinion appointment today. I'll give her a call."

She reached for her phone, and it rang in her hand. "Hello, Sara Ramsey speaking."

"Sara, it's Mavis, dear."

"Wow, we must be psychic. I had my phone in my hand, ready to ring you. How did you get on today?"

"The doctor examined the X-rays we took with us and said the same thing. He's given me three months. We've decided to take each day as it comes and are in the process of making a bucket list. There are several places I want to visit while I'm well enough to do it. So, we're going to hire a mobile home and travel around the country."

"Wow, yes, go for it. Sorry the news isn't better, lovely. Maybe getting away will do you some good, and you'll be able to prove them wrong. Dad loves his mobile home and getting away."

"Oh, yes. I forgot your father has one. Maybe he can give Ted some tips."

"I'm sure he'd be up for that. I'll ask him to give you a call. You know where we are if you need us, Mavis. Try to remain positive."

"You're so sweet. We do, and I'm determined not to give in to it. We'll have to see how that works out for us. Thank you for thinking about us. We love you more than you know."

Sara choked up at hearing the words. "We love you, too. We'll see you soon. Go and make life-changing plans together."

"We will. Enjoy the rest of your evening."

She jabbed the End Call button and threw the phone on the cushion beside her.

"I heard. That's devastating news for both of them. Glad they're going to make the most of the time they have left together."

"Poor Ted is not going to know what has hit him when she goes."

He picked up her hand and kissed the back of it. "We mustn't think about that. He knows we're here for him. We'll help him through it."

She smiled. "Thank you. You're amazing, Mark. I don't deserve you."

He pulled her closer and kissed her. "Hey, we deserve each other. I know we haven't had the best of times lately, but we got through the rough patch. It's onwards and upwards for us now."

"You and I, together, against the world."

"Steady on there, I don't think I'm as ambitious as you on that front."

They cleared up and had an early night. While Mark was in the bathroom, Sara sent Lorraine a text to see how things were progressing.

A text came back instantly: *We're leaving the scene now. I'll be in touch tomorrow. Nothing out of the ordinary found at the location.*

*Okay. Thanks for getting back to me. Speak soon.*

Without thinking, she added a heart to the end of her message.

Lorraine surprised her by sending one back as a response.

# 5

---

Sara was pleased to see Carla's car already at the station when she arrived the following morning. She said hello to the desk sergeant on the way through the reception area. "All quiet overnight, Jeff?"

"Not long got in myself, ma'am. Yes, it appears to have been a quiet one."

"Let me know if anything interesting comes your way."

He saluted. "I'll do that."

She walked up the stairs and into the incident room. Carla was staring at her computer screen.

"Good morning. Thanks for coming in early. Have you been here long?"

"Long enough for my coffee to go cold."

"I'll get you another one. How come? You seemed really focused on something when I came in."

"I've been doing some preliminary background checks on the second victim."

"And? Anything interesting come to light?"

"Hard to say yet. Nothing of significance, really."

"After I've held the morning meeting, I think you and I should take a trip out to the school."

"Any particular reason? I know it's what we usually do, but you have a certain look in your eye."

Sara laughed and made them both a drink. "There are no flies on you. Yes, we need to ask the relevant questions, but I also want to view the footage from their cameras to see if anyone at the school tampered with Alan's car."

"I thought you might. The same thing crossed my mind last night. I'm getting as bad as you regarding taking my work home with me. Des wasn't too impressed. He was expecting us to discuss the final touches that we need to sort out for the wedding. To be honest, I've had it up to here with it all." She raised her flat hand above her head.

"I told you what to do, but did you listen to me? Nope."

"I can't elope. If it were up to me, I would do it in a heartbeat, but his parents would go apeshit."

"Shame on them. It's your day, and the expense is laughable these days."

"Tell me about it. It's my folks who are expected to cover the costs. Mum and Dad can't afford it, although they're not telling me that right now. They keep saying that they've put money aside specifically for the occasion. I wish they'd spend the money on themselves."

"Maybe you should put your foot down if that's how you feel."

Carla groaned and shrugged. "What would be the point? I'm outnumbered."

"Then maybe Des and his family should chip in."

"Not their responsibility. I keep asking Des the same, and that's how he responds." She placed her hands over her face.

Sara quickly rushed over to comfort her. "Hey, you don't need all this stress, Carla. What you need to do is stand your ground and tell folks what you want on the day."

"I've tried." She pulled a tissue from the packet she kept in her drawer. "No one is listening to me. They're telling me it's wedding day jitters, but it's not."

Sara hugged her. "Oh bugger. There must be something you can do, Carla."

"There is... call it off. I'm tempted, believe me."

"You can't do that. Des would never forgive you, not at this late stage."

"Damned if I do and damned if I don't. It's too much for me to handle, Sara."

"My heart goes out to you. You're going to need to tell Des how you feel."

"I've tried. He changes the subject all the time."

Sara perched on the desk beside her partner, her heartstrings tugging at the dilemma facing her. "I'm sorry. I wish there was something I could do to help."

"As you were the one who set me up with Des in the first place, you could have a quiet word with him."

"What the...? It wouldn't be right, hon. Des and his family would think I'm interfering."

"Exactly. I'm between the devil and the deep blue sea, and I'm struggling to come up with a solution."

"It'll come to you when you're least expecting it. I'll try to think of something, as well."

"Thanks, Sara. What would I do without you?"

Sara grinned. "Probably suffer in silence. Now drink your coffee while it's hot. I'm going to clear some of my post. Let me know when everyone's here."

"I will."

Sara entered the office, paused to take in the view that was shrouded by cloud today, and then continued to her desk. She booted up her computer to find twenty-two emails awaiting her attention, but very few letters, which was a change. She got on with the task of answering her emails but grew bored with writing the same response to most of them, so she switched to opening her letters. One of them caught her attention, as it was handwritten.

·  ·  ·

*Do the right thing and investigate the past, or more will die.*


"CARLA, GET IN HERE."

Carla appeared in the doorway within seconds. "What is it?"

By this time Sara had withdrawn two gloves from her drawer. She threw one across the desk. "You'll need to put that on."

"I will? Why?"

Sara passed her the letter.

Carla snapped the glove in place and read the note. "What the fuck? That means the killer knows we're working the case. How?"

"He or she is watching us."

Carla ran a hand around her face. "Fuck, that's all we need, a looney on our tails, watching our every move."

"Shit happens. We're going to have to be extra vigilant during this investigation. Is everyone here?"

"We're waiting for Jill to arrive. She rang and said she's running a few minutes late as she had a flat tyre to deal with."

"That's a shame. We'll start without her; we need to get on. I'm going to give the press officer a call. I think I should hold a conference today, if only to stay ahead of this fucker."

"I agree. I'll get the board ready."

"Thanks. I'll be with you soon." Sara picked up her phone and rang Jane Donaldson. "Hey, it's your favourite detective inspector speaking."

"Hello, Kim, how are you?"

"What? It's Sara Ramsey."

Jane chuckled. "I know. I was messing with you."

"Well, don't." Sara laughed.

"What do you need? As if I don't know."

"Sorry to be so predictable. Is there any chance you can arrange a conference for this afternoon for me, please?"

"Consider it done. What time?"

"Around three would be perfect. We have a heavy morning ahead of us that might creep into the afternoon."

"I'll round them up for three. Anything I can do in the meantime?"

"I don't think so. Will you text me the confirmation?"

"Of course. See you later."

"Thanks, Jane." Sara ended the call, drank the final dregs of her coffee, then joined the others in the incident room.

Jill burst through the door as Sara drew everyone's attention.

"Sorry I'm late, boss. I got here as quickly as I could."

"At breakneck speed by the look of things. Are you all right? Craig, get Jill a coffee, will you?"

He bounced out of his chair.

"Thanks, Craig. I'm fine, boss. My neighbour came to my rescue and sorted the tyre out for me in a matter of minutes. I'd still be getting the wheel nuts off if it were down to me."

The team all laughed.

"You're here now. Right, here's what we have so far. The more observant amongst you will notice that Carla has added another name to the board."

Carla nodded and crossed the room to her desk.

Sara apprised them of the crime scene which she and Carla had attended the previous evening and then told the team what she expected of them during the day. "Right, Carla and I are going to nip out to the primary school where Alan worked. We'll ask the staff and head out there the usual questions. We're going to need to obtain any security footage they might have, as it's possible Alan's car was sabotaged. It all stinks of a premeditated crime. Craig, I've just received a note through the post. Can you run it over to the lab for me? I've put it in an evidence bag. It's on my desk. Ask them to check for fingerprints and also get them to compare the writing, just to make sure we're dealing with the same perpetrator. If we're not, then that's a different ballgame that we're going to have to deal with."

"Leave it with me, boss. Shall I shoot it over to the lab now?"

"After the meeting will do. What I need from the rest of you is to carry out the usual checks on both victims. Carla, you mentioned that you'd found something earlier. Care to share with the team what that was?"

"I found a weak connection between them. They were on some kind of committee together about twenty years ago."

"Okay, let's bear that in mind for the future, if nothing else comes our way in the meantime. Okay, let's crack on with our tasks. I should think Carla and I will be out until lunchtime at least. If you uncover anything of importance, call me."

SARA SWITCHED off the engine after they drew up in the car park of the primary school. The receptionist was busy typing. She had headphones on and wasn't aware that they had arrived. Sara waved from several directions to gain her attention.

Embarrassed, the receptionist whipped off the headphones and approached the desk. "I'm so sorry. Once I get caught up in my work, everything else pales into insignificance. "How can I help?"

Sara smiled and showed her ID. "DI Sara Ramsey. We'd like to speak to the head, if that's possible."

"Oh my. The police. Ah, right, let me check her schedule. I think she has a couple of Zoom meetings booked in for this morning." She picked up a clipboard and ran her finger down a list, then peered at her watch. "She should be free to see you. I'll check with her." The receptionist walked up the corridor and knocked on a door about twenty feet away. She entered the room and returned to her station a few seconds later. "Yes, Mrs Ward will see you now. Please, come with me."

"Thanks," Sara replied.

They followed her up the corridor, past lots of colourful pictures the kids had drawn, pinned to the walls on either side.

Mrs Ward remained seated as they entered. "Hello. Please, take a seat. Would you like a drink?"

"No, we're fine. Thank you for agreeing to see us."

"Not at all. I'm intrigued to know how I can help."

Sara and Carla sat in the chairs opposite the headmistress.

"It's about one of your teachers, Alan Fletcher," Sara said.

Mrs Ward, who was in her mid-forties, steepled her fingers together and tilted her head. She frowned and asked, "What about him?"

"Has his husband not called you this morning?" Sara was puzzled by the way the head matter-of-factly asked her question.

"No. I'm confused, why would he?"

"Sorry, I just assumed that by now you would have known what happened after Alan left school last night."

"I don't. Please, tell me what you're talking about."

"I'm sorry to have to tell you that Alan was killed yesterday."

Her hands slammed onto the table, and the colour drained from her cheeks. "He what? How? Did he die in an accident?"

"We believe someone intentionally targeted him. Now I'm confused. Didn't you realise he was missing today?"

"No. He booked the day off. He said he had a dentist's appointment with Joe." She ran a hand around her face. "This is terrible. Why would he have been targeted, as you suggested?"

"That's what we need to find out. Has he ever had any problems with any of the other teachers here at the school?"

Mrs Ward shook her head.

"What about any of the kids' parents?"

"No. He was a really easy-going chap. Everyone enjoyed working with him and, as for the kids, they absolutely idolised him. I can't believe this has happened. I don't want to know the ins and outs of the crime but please, tell me he didn't suffer before his death."

"I can't tell you that. We believe he was followed home last night and suspect that his car might have been tampered with, causing him to break down en route. He was found tied to a tree with several injuries to his body."

Tears welled up in her eyes. "Oh no. This is terrible. Why would anyone do such a wicked thing to such a nice man?"

"That's what we're desperate to find out. Is there any chance we could view the footage from your CCTV here at the school?"

"You believe the killer struck here?"

"It's the only logical explanation we can come up with at this time."

"Let's find out then. Come with me. I'll see if I can get the machine working for you. If not, I know I can call on Mr Davies to help me."

They left the room and walked the length of the corridor. Mrs Ward switched the light on in a smaller room. The equipment was pretty basic. She turned on the monitor while Sara and Carla collected three chairs from a stack in the corner.

"Right, let's see if we can get this to function."

Within seconds, Mrs Ward had worked her magic and produced an image on the screen. "How far back would you like me to go?"

"Obviously, we believe the incident happened sometime yesterday."

"Rightio. There is a week's worth of filming on each of the discs, so let's see what we can find. This is the car park at the front of the school. Most of the teachers tend to park there. Yes, that's Alan's car, over by the exit. It was his pride and joy, the cleanest vehicle in the car park most days. He put most of the other teachers, including me, to shame. This was at three in the afternoon. Let me whizz backwards through the day."

"If you wouldn't mind. That would be great."

"Okay, let's go back. The camera has a good view of his vehicle. Hang on, what's this?"

They watched a hooded figure walk past Alan's car and then retrace their steps. Keeping an eye on everything going on around them, the person ducked down beside the car and made their way to its rear.

"Is there any chance you can zoom in for us, Mrs Ward?" Sara asked. She stood and got closer to the monitor but then needed to take a step back as Mrs Ward managed to zoom in, and the image hurt her eyes. "Okay, he seems to be tampering with the exhaust."

"It looks like he's shoving something up it. Is it a rag of sorts?" Carla asked.

"I'll rewind it," Mrs Ward said.

The image went back and forth a few times.

"I think we've seen enough. Can we get a copy of this, Mrs Ward?"

"Of course, if I can figure out how to do it."

Carla stood and helped her. "I think it's this button here. Yes, that's right."

"Yes, gosh, I'm glad you're here. I wouldn't have had a clue. Do you think this person is the one who killed Alan?"

"It's possible. Unless he had an accomplice. We won't know until we find out who this person is. Have you seen anyone hanging around the school lately?"

"No, not at all. We're off the beaten track as it were, so there's really no need for any traffic or members of the public to come out this way. This doesn't seem good, does it?"

"No, I think it's obvious what this person's intentions were and who they were targeting."

Mrs Ward slipped the disc into a plastic sleeve and handed it to Sara. "If there's anything else I can help with, please reach out."

"We'll leave you to it. If you could let the other members of staff know and tell them to be extra vigilant over the next few days, just to be on the safe side."

"I'll ask them if Alan had confided in them and get back to you if I hear anything."

"We can't ask for more than that. Thank you. I'm sorry we had to deliver the awful news to you today."

"He will be missed not only by the other members of staff but also by the pupils. He would often stay behind and help run special activities for some of the children."

"I should have asked, how long had Alan worked at the school?"

"For the last five years. He found his calling to be a teacher later in life. He was forty-eight."

"Ah, I see. Do you know what his previous job was?"

"He was an accountant. He told me he loathed it come the end and was desperate to work with children. He wanted to lead them on the right path for their future. He specifically loved working with the kids who struggled with reading and writing. He had a lot of patience. His willingness to let them shine blew me away. He would work with children individually, whilst still being on call for the rest of the kids in the class. Most teachers won't entertain doing that these days. I mean it—he was one of the best teachers I've ever worked with." Tears emerged once more, and she swiped them away. "Well, this isn't going to get us anywhere, is it?"

She led the way out of the room, and they parted at the reception desk.

Sara gave her one of her business cards. "Call me day or night if you hear anything out of the ordinary."

"I will. You have my word. I hope you track down this person. I feel gutted that it happened in our car park."

Sara smiled. "We appreciate your help and the footage you've supplied us with. Take care."

They left the building.

Sara walked over to the spot where Alan had parked his car the day before and surveyed the area. "I hadn't realised it before, but this is a dead end, which means the person must have come in the same way we did."

Carla glanced around and pointed to a path over to her right. "Not necessarily. There's a footpath over there. They might have parked their car on the other side, knowing that the school was bound to have CCTV. They could have accessed the area via the footpath."

"Bummer, you're right. What does that tell us?"

"That his intention was clear. Or, at least, that the sabotage was premeditated."

Sara nodded as she mulled over what they should do next. "Totally. He used to be an accountant. We need to find out where and do some digging with that firm, too."

"Do you want to go back and ask?"

"No, we'll return to base. You can ring Mrs Ward en route and ask her to send me a copy of Alan's CV. She's bound to have it on record with his application for the job."

"Good thinking."

"It's all we've got at the moment." Sara pressed her key fob, and the doors clunked open.

She pulled out of the car park, and Carla rang the school and asked to speak to Mrs Ward. Unfortunately, she was on another call, so Carla left a message with the receptionist, who promised to pass it on to Mrs Ward when she was free.

By the time they got back to the station, the headmistress had sent Sara an email. She opened it in her office and printed off the attachment, which was Alan's CV. She read it through. Nothing in it raised any alarm bells. She set it aside and joined the rest of the team. They went through what they had discovered that morning, which wasn't much.

"Jill, what about the socials? Any disagreements on there that we should know about for either of the victims?"

"I haven't stumbled across anything of that nature, not yet, boss."

"So, it looks like we're going to be reliant on the press conference this afternoon."

"And the DNA on the notes," Carla added.

"Yep, talking of which, I'm going to have to jot down a few notes in preparation for the conference, but first, Craig, I need you to check through the CCTV and ANPRs in the area. When we were out at the school today, we noticed the road in which it is located is a dead end, although Carla spotted a footpath that the killer might have used before he tampered with Alan's car. Can you find out where that leads to and see if there are any cameras around there?"

"I'll get on that right away."

"Let's widen the search. I'm guessing the killer must have followed Alan during his journey home. Barry, why don't you team up with Craig again? Hopefully, we can get the results quicker with two of you on the task."

"I'm up for it, boss," Barry replied.

"I'll be in my office for the next half an hour. Carla, would you mind nipping out to the baker's to pick up lunch for us?"

"Not at all."

She left Carla taking down everyone's orders and returned to her office. She had almost completed the notes she wanted to make when Carla appeared with her lunch. "I bought you a tuna mayo on brown. This is on me. You bought the last one."

"Thanks. It wasn't a hint, sending you to get the lunch."

"I know. I'm going to make a coffee. Do you want one?"

"That would be great."

Carla delivered her coffee moments later.

Sara set her notes aside and started on her sandwich just as her office phone rang. She finished her mouthful and answered it on the fourth ring. "DI Sara Ramsey. How may I help?"

"Hello, Inspector. I expected you to answer more quickly than that."

She frowned, not recognising the voice. "Sorry, who is this?"

The caller laughed. "I suppose it's too soon for my voice to be familiar. It's DCI Blake."

"Oh, sorry, sir. Yes, far too early. Is there something I can do for you?"

"I'm checking in to see how things are progressing with your investigation."

"Umm... it's trying, like most investigations in the preliminary stages. It's too early for us to have uncovered anything significant." Sara wanted to ask what he was expecting from her so soon into the investigation, but she held her tongue.

"Ah, yes. Earlier, I received a call from a Nigel Manning. He seemed a feisty individual."

"He's the son of the first victim. I'm sensing he put in a complaint about me."

"He didn't get a chance to. I cut him off before he made any demands."

"Oh, I see. Any reason, sir?"

"Because I don't take kindly to people criticising members of my team, especially when they have an exemplary record like you."

Sara's cheeks flushed. "Thank you, sir. That means a lot to me." She might have said it, but after the words came out, she kicked herself for being so foolish. She'd been in this situation before with his predecessor. She was adamant she wouldn't drop her guard with a senior officer in the future. Keeping her distance was going to be paramount in her mind after what she'd experienced with Price.

"What's on your agenda today?"

"Well, unfortunately, we're now investigating two murders which we believe might be connected."

"So, Manning's father was the first victim, and now you're dealing with a second one?"

*Doh! Yeah!* "That's right. We're doing all we can to find a connection between the two men."

"Wait, what makes you think there's a connection?"

"The killer left a note at both scenes."

"Could it be a copycat killer?" he asked.

Sara shook her head as if he were in the room with her. "I don't see how that's possible because nothing has appeared in the press yet about the Manning murder. I'm about to hold a conference in the next thirty minutes."

"Ah, I see what you mean. Would you like me to attend? It might keep the wolves at bay if your DCI puts his weight behind the investigation."

"I haven't needed the support from my senior officer in the past... er, I mean, not in that respect. She always left me to it."

"Don't get me wrong, I'm not saying you're not capable of holding a conference by yourself."

"Good, because in my twenty years on the Force, I've held hundreds of successful conferences," she snapped.

"I don't doubt it, Inspector. All I was suggesting is that this could turn out to be an ideal time for us to show a united front, given all the adverse publicity the station has received lately."

"Ah, I'm with you. You'd prefer to make this conference all about the station and your appointment as DCI, rather than trying to gain information about the two victims and their families." She winced and closed her eyes, waiting for the backlash.

"Not at all. I'll take a step back and let you deal with the press, then."

"I'd prefer that. Thank you, sir. I didn't mean to come across as..."

"There's no need for you to apologise. I completely understand how betrayed you must feel right now. However, I want you to know that I'm a good man, a straight officer. I haven't taken, and I have no intention of taking, any backhanders from any scumbag criminals, unlike Price. All I'm asking is for you to give me a fair crack of the whip."

Sara smiled. "Okay. If you're willing to do the same."

"If I were in the room with you, I'd shake your hand. It's a deal. Glad we're on the same page."

"We are."

"Keep me informed about the investigation, and don't hesitate to ask for help if you need it."

"I won't. Thank you. And, sir..."

"Yes, Inspector."

"It was nothing personal."

"I appreciate that. I'd better get back to this blasted paperwork now."

Sara ended the call and glanced at her watch. She had another ten minutes before meeting Jane in the anteroom. She checked in with the team, who were all still hard at it.

"How's it going?"

Craig raised his hand.

She crossed the room to speak to him and Barry. "Have you found anything?"

"We've located Alan's car and kept it under observation. A few other vehicles followed him home but turned off before he took the road where you and Carla found him. This BMW gets close to him at one stage but then appears to allow the other cars to get between them."

"Okay." Sara peered at the screen. "I don't suppose you've got a registration number on it, have you?"

Craig tutted and shook his head. "No, it was covered in mud. I'm going to search for a list of all the black BMWs in the area."

"Thank you. I was about to suggest the same. Right, it's time for me to face the press. Wish me luck."

She left the room and made her way down the stairs to meet Jane Donaldson. "Hi, how are you? Thanks for pulling this off at short notice."

"Nothing new there," Jane said. "I'm fine. More to the point, how are you? I know how much you detest facing the journalists."

"Actually, I'm quite chilled about it. We need to get the word out about these two murders, and this is the only way we're going to do it."

"I'll be right beside you. I'm ready when you are."

"Let's get it over with."

Sara followed Jane onto the stage, adjusted the microphone stand and took a deep breath. The press room at Hereford Station was packed to the gills with journalists and cameras and held an air of anticipation. Sara's steely gaze swept across the room, briefly settling on some of the more familiar faces before she began.

"Good morning, everyone," she said, her voice calm and determined, but laced with authority. "Thank you for being here today. We are currently investigating two tragic, violent murders that will no doubt send shockwaves through our community."

Sara paused, allowing the murmurs in the room to die down. Off to the right, she spotted DCI Blake, and her nerves jangled. He smiled and gave an encouraging nod.

"I can't go into specific details of the crimes. However, I can give you the names of the victims and where they were found. The first victim, Richard Manning, a solicitor, was discovered in his office early Tuesday morning. The killer left behind a chilling scene. At this time, we believe Mr Manning may have been specifically targeted, but the exact motive for the attack remains unclear. Our team is working tirelessly to uncover the circumstances that led to his death."

Sara's words hung in the air. The room fell silent except for the scratching of pens on notepads.

"The second victim," Sara continued, "was Alan Fletcher, a well-respected primary school teacher. Mr Fletcher's vehicle had been sabotaged, which forced him to stop on a remote road near Eaton Bishop. There, he was brutally attacked. His injuries were severe and ultimately led to his death. Someone cruelly left him to die in the woods. The nature of this crime was both calculated and callous."

A reporter raised her hand, and Sara gestured for her to speak.

"DI Ramsey, is there any connection between the victims?"

Sara took a moment to consider her words. "At this stage, we are exploring all possible links. Both Mr Manning and Mr Fletcher were upstanding members of the community. Their deaths are a significant loss not only to their families but also to their colleagues. However, it is too early to confirm any connection between them. At this time, we ask for patience as we continue our investigation."

Another journalist spoke up. "Are you treating this as the work of a serial killer?"

Sara's expression hardened slightly. "We are not ruling out any possibilities, but it would be premature to make such assumptions. What I can tell you is that these crimes were heinous acts of violence, and we are fully committed to finding and punishing those responsible."

She glanced at Jane, who stepped forward to place a map of Hereford and Eaton Bishop on the easel beside the podium. On it, the key locations related to the murders had been marked, drawing the attention of the press.

"We are appealing to the public for any information that could assist us," Sara said. "Did you see anything unusual near Mr Manning's office on Ford Street on Monday night? Or near the woods in Eaton Bishop around the time of Mr Fletcher's death the following evening? Even the smallest detail could be crucial."

Sara's tone softened slightly as she concluded. "Our hearts go out to the families of Mr Manning and Mr Fletcher. I want to assure them and the residents of Hereford that we will not rest until justice is served. Thank you."

As Sara stepped back from the podium, a flurry of questions erupted from the reporters. She exchanged a glance with Jane, who gave her a subtle nod of approval. The hunt for the killer had only just begun, but Sara's resolve, she hoped, would be unshakeable.

DCI Blake joined Sara and Jane in the anteroom. He applauded her. "You were the utter professional out there."

Her cheeks warmed up. "Thank you, sir. I was surprised to see you here. Jane, have you met my new boss, DCI Blake?"

He shook hands with the press officer. "I promise not to make a habit of showing up out of the blue."

"I'm glad to hear it," Sara said.

"Sara has always played a major role in these conferences. In that regard, she's one of the most professional officers the station has to offer," Jane said.

"I can see that. I'll leave you to it, ladies."

They watched him leave, and then Sara let out a huge sigh.

"I thought I was going to dry up when I spotted him in the room."

"Thank God you didn't react. The journalists would have jumped all over you."

"I know. I feel like he was checking up on me."

"He seems a nice chap. Cut him some slack. He's probably trying to find his feet."

"Yeah. Let's hope he doesn't make a habit of stepping on mine during the process."

They both laughed.

# 6

Regrettably, it wasn't until the following morning that they received a response from the conference. Sara was attending to her post when the call came in. Jill rang her.

"Sorry to interrupt you, boss. I have a woman on the phone who is keen to speak with you."

"Can you take a message, and I'll call her back?"

"I don't think she'll accept that, sorry. She was pretty insistent that she would only speak to you."

Sara sighed. A pile of paperwork had landed on her desk overnight, and she was keen to make headway on it without being distracted. "Pass her through. Thanks, Jill."

"Doing it now. She wouldn't give me her name."

"Hello, are you there?" the woman sounded irate.

"Hello. You've been transferred. I'm DI Sara Ramsey. How may I help?"

"Oh, I see. Umm... sorry for sounding off. I'm apprehensive about making this call."

Her words sparked Sara's intrigue. "Please, don't be. I'm a very easy-going person. What did you want to talk to me about?"

"The press conference you held yesterday. I watched it last night... it stirred up a lot of memories."

"It did? May I ask in what respect?"

"I know the two murdered victims you mentioned."

"You do? How?"

"I can't tell you that."

"Can I have your name?"

After a few moments' pause, she said, "It's Amanda Keller. You need to delve into the past. That's all I'm prepared to say at this time."

"Wait, don't hang up. Please, we're struggling to get the investigation going. If you know anything that might help us... please share it with me."

"I don't, not really. I'm sorry, I thought I was doing the right thing calling you... I'm not so sure now. I have to go."

"No, please, let's meet up and discuss this. What if more people are killed? Will you be able to live with yourself, knowing that you might have prevented it?"

"This isn't about me. It's about what they did. My conscience is clear. It always has been."

"Clear about what? Please, if you know what this is about, you have to tell me. Think of the families who have lost a loved one."

"I am. Believe me, I am. I have to go. I've given you a clue. It's up to you to figure it out now."

"Please don't go. You haven't told me enough to make a difference. How do you know the two men? What were they guilty of?"

The line went dead, and Sara slammed her fist onto the desk.

CARLA WAS FLICKING through some post that had arrived for the team when she stumbled upon a handwritten one with her name on the front. She glanced up to see if the others had noticed. They hadn't. She opened the letter and read the short note.

YOU'RE PERSONALLY CLOSER *to the truth than you think.*

. . .

SHE TUCKED the note back into the envelope and went to the ladies'. There, she removed her phone from her pocket and rang her father.

"Hello, Carla. Fancy you ringing me at this time of the day. Are you on a day off?"

"No. I'm at work, Dad. Did you see the news yesterday?"

"I didn't. Why? I was busy decorating the spare room. Your aunt is coming in a few weeks, and your mother has been nagging me to freshen it up before she comes. Things came to a head yesterday; I've been procrastinating for weeks. Your mother kicked my butt, and off we trotted to the DIY store. She chose the paint, of course. I would have gone for something totally different from the one she picked. Anyway, to get back to your point, no, I haven't seen the news. Don't tell me you were on it, were you?"

"No, but Sara was. She put out an appeal to the general public about an investigation we're working on. The thing is, I did some research yesterday, and something pricked a memory, but I need you to verify something for me."

"Sounds ominous. What's this about, love?"

"Do the names Alan Fletcher and Richard Manning mean anything to you?"

Her father fell quiet.

She checked if they were still connected. "Dad? Are you still there?"

"Yes, I'm here." His response was subdued.

"What can you tell me about them, Dad?"

"I'd rather not discuss it. Why have those particular names surfaced?"

Carla tutted. "You're kidding me. I need to know what happened in the past."

"Lots of things. That's why it's called the past. And to be honest with you, that's where it belongs, in the past."

"No, Dad, you're going to tell me. If you don't, I'm going to pass the information I know to Sara, my boss. You won't be able to brush her aside like you're trying to do to me."

"Why have those names come up?" he pressed her.

"Because they're both *dead*, that's why. We're investigating their murders. Now tell me, what do you know about this?"

"Shit! Is this some kind of wind-up?"

"As if I would joke about two members of the public losing their lives. What do you know about them?" All she could hear was her father breathing heavily on the line. She left it a moment before she prompted him for an answer. "Dad, for God's sake, tell me!"

"I can't."

"Shit, if you won't confide in your own daughter... Jesus, if you're involved in this, then your life could be in danger. There's more..."

"What do you mean, there's more?"

"I've just opened a letter here that was addressed to me personally. I rarely, if ever, get post at work."

"And what did it say?" her father whispered.

"'You're personally closer to the truth than you think.' That's why I'm calling you. You have to tell me what you know... now."

She heard a thump and then a groan.

"Dad. Dad. Are you all right?"

Her father cried out for help.

"I'll get an ambulance. Don't move. Is Mum there with you?"

"No. She's out."

"I'm going to hang up. I'll call the ambulance and then come over there myself. I love you, Dad." She ended the call, rang nine-nine-nine and requested an ambulance to go to her father's address, then ran back to tell Sara that she was leaving.

She barged into Sara's office, her heart racing and pounding violently against her ribs. "Sara, I have to go. I think my father is having a heart attack."

Sara flew out of her chair. "I'll drive you. You can't get behind the wheel, not in that state. Did he call you?"

"I was on the phone to him. Please, I've got to get to the house. We're wasting time."

Sara grabbed her jacket from the back of the chair. "How far is it?"

"Ten minutes, if that, if we use the siren."

"What are we waiting for?"

THEY ARRIVED at the house seconds before the ambulance got there. Carla used her spare key to open the front door. Sara followed her into the house but left the front door ajar for the paramedics.

"Dad, where are you?" Carla ran from room to room downstairs and finally found her father in the conservatory, lying on the floor. "Shit! Are you okay?"

"No. I can't breathe properly."

Carla undid his top shirt button.

Sara entered the room behind her. "I'll keep an ear open for the ambulance. How are you, sir?"

"Hello, Sara. I've had better days. My chest and arm hurt. Am I having a heart attack?"

"Stick with us, Dad. The ambulance is just outside."

"I'll tell them to hurry up," Sara said and sprinted out of the room.

Carla leaned forward, kissed her father's sweaty forehead and whispered, "I'm sorry. I should never have told you. I was worried about you."

"Let's not talk about it now, love. Keep your mother safe while I'm in hospital." He cried out in pain as the two paramedics and Sara entered the room.

"Stand back," the male paramedic ordered Carla.

She hurriedly crawled away from her father and got to her feet beside Sara. They clung to each other, tears rolling down their faces while they watched the paramedics attend to her father. They attached him to a monitor with tabs fixed to his chest and then quickly moved him onto a stretcher and out of the house.

"We'll follow you," Sara shouted.

"Do that. See you at A and E."

Carla was standing there, dumbstruck, staring after the ambulance as it drew away. "I need to call my mother. Heck, what the hell do I tell her?"

"The truth. Do you want me to tell her instead?"

"No. I'll do it. She might get too worked up hearing the news from a stranger. No offence."

"None taken. Do it in the car. We should get on the road."

Carla nodded and rushed back to secure the house. She slipped her key back into her purse, then jumped back into the car.

"I hope he makes it," Carla said.

"He will. He's in safe hands. Get on the phone to your mother. She'll be furious if she finds out you delayed calling her."

Carla rang her mother's number. It went to voicemail. "Shit. Hi, Mum, it's Carla. Can you ring me straight back? It's important."

"Did your father say where she was?"

"He might have done. I've forgotten. Damn, why Dad? Why now?"

"Has he been under any stress lately?"

Carla shook her head and then realised that Sara wouldn't have seen her. "Sorry, no. He mentioned he was going to decorate the spare room for when my aunt comes to stay." She didn't have the heart to tell Sara the truth, not when only the bare facts were at her disposal. *What a frigging mess. Please, please, don't take him from us, not yet.*

She rang her mother every five minutes until finally she got to speak to her in person. "Bloody hell, Mum, where are you?"

"I was in a bad reception area. I'm in town, doing some shopping. What's wrong? I've just looked, and I have about fifteen missed calls from you."

"It's Dad. He's on his way to the hospital. Sara and I are following the ambulance."

"What? Did something happen? I told him those ladders weren't safe and to buy a new set."

"No, it's nothing like that. Just get to the hospital, now, Mum. Please, drive carefully."

"Oh my God. Okay, I'll get a taxi, I don't think I'll be able to drive. I'm too worked up."

"Whatever. Go to A and E. I'll meet you there. I love you."

Her mother started crying. "I love you, too. Is he going to be okay, Carla?"

"I don't know. I hope so."

"I'm flagging a taxi down now. I should be there soon. How far out are you?"

"About two minutes. See you there." Carla ended the call before her mother could continue the conversation from the taxi, knowing how much she would grill her until she revealed the truth.

Sara reached over and grasped her hand. "He's going to be all right. You have to keep believing that, Carla."

A single tear dripped onto her cheek. "How do you know that? None of us know what state his heart is in at this stage. What if he's already dead?"

"He's not. The paramedics would have pulled over and told us if that were the case. You're going to have to remain strong, if only for your mother's sake."

"What about for my sake?" she snapped back. "I'm sorry, that was uncalled for. I can't cope with this. He's only fifty-six. That's far too young to be having a bloody heart attack. What if he doesn't survive? How will Mum cope on her own?"

"He's not going anywhere. You need to get those thoughts out of your mind. And, if the worst does happen, your mum will survive and so will you. It's part of life, dealing with grief. Believe me, it's not going to be easy... what am I saying? Let's not write him off yet. He's a reasonably fit man, isn't he? He looked it."

"Yes. He walks the dog three to four miles a day, so he has that on his side."

"There you go then. Keep faith in him. Like I said, your mother is going to need you to be strong for her. Don't crumble now. You'll be no use to anyone, love."

Carla wrung her hands in her lap, then inhaled and exhaled a few calming breaths to put her back on track. "I know. Just to warn you, Mum is going to be a wreck when we see her."

"It's to be expected. They've been together longer than you've been alive. Keep that in mind. Don't be too hard on her. So what if she's emotional? She has a right to be in the circumstances."

"Thank you for the lecture. Not that I needed one."

"For goodness' sake. I wasn't lecturing you. I was merely pointing out the facts."

"Facts that I'm well aware of. Back off, Sara." She turned to look out of the side window but realised her mistake and closed her eyes as more tears threatened. "I'm sorry. I shouldn't have spoken to you like that. Please forgive me."

"It's forgotten about. You can use me as a verbal punching bag anytime you like when we're alone."

"Thank you. I'm worried about him and how Mum is going to react when she gets to see him."

"Like any other wife who has been with her husband for a long time. All you can do is be there for her, supporting her."

"I will. God, we're nearly there."

"I'll drop you off and park in the usual spot if I can get a space."

"I'll pay the fee."

"We'll argue the toss about that later. It's not important."

Sara drew up and dropped her partner off. Carla jogged over to the ambulance and watched the two paramedics unload her father. "Dad, how are you?"

"I can't tell you that, love. I think I'm all right, but who knows what's around the corner?"

"Mum's on her way. We'll get to see you when we can. Stay strong."

He squeezed her hand and mumbled, "Take care of your mother. She's going to be beside herself."

Carla bent to kiss her father.

"Stand back," the male paramedic instructed.

They whisked him through the main doors to the A and E department. She watched them, frozen to the spot, until Sara joined her not long after.

Sara slotted her arm through Carla's. "Come on, let's grab a coffee inside while we wait for your mum to arrive."

"I can't. It wouldn't stay down. You go ahead if you want one. Hang on, here's a taxi. I think it's her."

Her mother got out of the back of the taxi, paid the driver and ran towards them with tears streaming down her cheeks. "Where is he?"

"They've taken him in. We won't be able to see him, not yet, Mum." Carla hugged her mother, but her mum pulled out of the embrace.

"We should be inside in case they call us to be with him."

"They've only just taken him in, Mum. That's not likely to happen for a while. Why don't we have a drink while we wait?"

Her mother shrugged and marched through the front door. The reception desk was directly ahead of them. Bypassing the café, she strode purposefully towards the receptionist and announced her arrival. "I'm Mrs Jameson. My husband was brought in by ambulance not long ago. Can I find out what's happening to him?"

"If you'd like to take a seat, someone will be out to speak with you soon once he's been assessed," the receptionist told her with a smile.

"And how long is that going to be?"

"However long it takes to assess your husband."

"Mum, let's do as the lady asks and take a seat. They're doing the best they can for him."

"Are they?" her mother snapped, shrugging Carla's arm off.

Carla groaned and put her hands on her mother's shoulders. She guided her to a nearby seat.

"I'll grab us some drinks. What would you like, Mrs Jameson?" Sara asked.

"To know how my husband is," she bit back.

"I'm sure someone will be out to update you shortly. In the meantime, how about a nice cup of tea?"

"Yes, okay. Milk with one sugar. Thank you."

Carla rolled her eyes, silently apologising to Sara. "I'll have a coffee. Here's some money. We don't expect you to pay for it, Sara."

"Keep it. You can get the next one." Sara walked back towards the café.

"Are you all right, Mum?" Carla asked. She slipped her hand over her mother's.

"I don't know, am I? What happened? I'm confused about your involvement in this. Did you go and pester him for some money for the wedding?"

"No. I would never do that. I'm appalled you should think that of me."

Her mother's chin dipped and trembled. "I'm sorry. I'm worried about him and I'm not thinking straight." She checked her phone. "I haven't got a missed call from him. Why did he call you before he called me?"

"He didn't. I was on the phone to him when he fell. Sara drove me over to the house. I used my spare key to get in and found him lying on the cold floor in the conservatory. Thank goodness I rang for an ambulance before I left the station. He was in a sorry state when we arrived. The paramedics got there not long after."

"Oh my. What's wrong with him? Why isn't anyone telling me that?"

Sara arrived with the drinks and handed them around.

Carla sighed. "I think it was his heart."

"What?" Her mother twisted in her seat to face Carla. "He's a fit man. He shouldn't be having problems with his heart, not at his age."

Carla shrugged. "It happens, Mum. Who knows what goes on with our bodies? They're complex entities that have been known to flummox doctors over the years."

"You do talk a lot of twaddle. I know your father inside and out. If there was anything wrong with his heart, he would have told me."

Carla sat back and rested her head against the wall.

Sara nudged her and whispered in her ear, "She didn't mean it. She's worried about him. Don't take it personally."

Closing her eyes, Carla nodded.

*If I hadn't called him about the murders, this would never have happened. Did Dad have a bad heart already? Have I brought this on? Shit, I don't know what to do for the best. Mum would kill me if she found out I had something to do with this. Fuck, how is Sara going to react when I eventually share the news with her? I'm stuck in the middle, caught between a rock and a hard place. Please survive, Dad. I can't lose you now without knowing the truth. I know that sounds selfish, and I don't mean it to be, but the truth will help save further lives from being lost. I hope.*

Something sharp jabbed in Carla's side.

"It's the doctor. He's coming this way," her mother said.

They all jumped out of their seats.

"Please, sit down," the doctor suggested. "I appreciate how worried you must be about Mr Jameson. I wanted to make you aware of the situation before I go any further."

"How is my husband? Please tell me it's not his heart."

"I'm sorry, I can't tell you that. It is his heart. We're monitoring him at the moment."

"Was it a heart attack?" Carla asked.

"Yes. From what we can gather, he suffered a minor heart attack, if there is such a thing. Calling the ambulance when you did saved his life."

"Thank you, Doctor. That's a relief to know. What happens now?" Carla asked. She gripped her mother's hand and squeezed it tightly.

"He'll be monitored for the next twenty-four hours. Obviously, we're going to need to admit him for a few days. We'll run some tests on his heart once he feels more settled. Right now, he's feeling scared and unsure of what's going on. Maybe one of you could reassure him."

"It should be you, Mum. He'll listen to you."

"Are you up for it?" the doctor asked Carla's mother.

She shrugged and chewed her lip. "What if I break down and cry in front of him?"

"Don't, Mum. He's going to be relying on you to be tough for him, at least for now. Go on, you can do it."

Her mother covered her face with her hands, then dropped them and shook her arms out. "Okay, if I have to."

"Excellent news. If you'd like to come this way," the doctor said.

Her mother hesitated before Carla gave her a friendly push in the back. "Send him my love."

"I will," her mother called over her shoulder as she scurried along the corridor after the doctor.

"I hate to say this, but we're going to have to get back to the investigation soon," Sara said.

Carla nodded and placed her head in her hands. "I know. Maybe I should take the day off and be here for Mum."

"If that's what you want to do."

"I don't. However, in the circumstances, I think it might be the right thing to do."

"I agree. I'll leave you to it. Give my love to your father. Wish him a speedy recovery from me when you eventually see him."

Carla reached out and clutched Sara's hand. With tears in her eyes, she whispered, "I will, if he survives."

Sara flung an arm around her neck. "Don't be so ridiculous, of course he's going to survive. Hey, what's wrong with you? Where's your fighting spirit gone? This isn't like you, Carla. I know this has come as a shock to you, but you're tougher than this, usually. What's really going on? Is it the wedding? Are you thinking your dad won't make it to walk you down the aisle?"

Carla shook her head and stared at her clenched hands. "No, it's nothing like that." She removed the note, which she had slipped into a plastic bag, from her jacket pocket and passed it to Sara.

"What the fu...? What is this?"

"I received it in the post this morning. I went to the loo and rang my dad, seeking answers and..."

"That's when he had the heart attack," Sara finished off for her.

"Yes. He's in this condition because I had the audacity to confront him about the past."

"And what did your father say?"

"He didn't, not really. His heart started playing up the second I mentioned that someone had contacted me through the post. I haven't got the foggiest idea what the heck is going on, Sara. But one thing is certain: my father is involved."

Sara ran a hand through her hair. "Shit, shit, shit! Okay, I'm going to request that an officer is stationed outside his room at all times. Is there somewhere else your mother can stay in the meantime until we find this bastard?"

"Yes, I think she could stay with a friend. Oh God, how do I tell her?"

"You don't, not in so many words. I'll think of something, trust me."

Carla smiled weakly. It was all she could summon up at that moment. "What was my father involved in? And why, if it happened decades ago, is it only resurfacing now?"

"I don't know, but I intend to get to the bottom of it. Thank you for confiding in me. I appreciate it couldn't have been easy for you to reveal the truth."

"Is it the truth? I don't know. What if Dad's condition has nothing to do with that note? What then?"

"We'll find out soon enough. I'll go back to the station and start digging into the article you found that might link your father and the other two victims. I'd prefer it if you stayed here with him for now. I'll arrange for an officer to guard his room. It'll give you all some peace of mind. Try to encourage your mother to stay with a friend without alerting her."

"I think having an officer on guard outside Dad's room will frighten the life out of her."

"Shit. Okay, just tell her I've insisted on having someone there as a precaution."

"She's not stupid, Sara. She's going to realise something bad is going on."

"Okay, then. I'll leave it up to you what you tell her. You know her better than I do. I'll call you if we find anything."

"Thanks. I'm sorry to cause you so much trouble."

Sara stood, leaned in and kissed Carla on the cheek. "You haven't. Take care. Let me know as soon as you hear what the doctor has to say. I'll send the officer here to find you."

"I'll call you later. Thanks again. You're a good friend as well as an outstanding boss. I don't tell you that enough."

Sara waved her hand. "Get out of here. You'd do the same if you were in my position."

"I doubt it, but that's another story."

SARA WALKED up the corridor and peered over her shoulder as she reached the front door. She waved, unsure whether Carla would be looking or not. She paid for her ticket, which she'd take out of petty cash, then drove back to the station to fill in the rest of the team. She stopped off to speak to Jeff and apprised him of the situation. Shocked, he ordered a uniformed officer, who was passing through the reception area at the time, to go to the hospital and seek out Carla.

She smiled. "You're a good man. Thanks, Jeff."

"Only doing my job, ma'am. How is Carla's father?"

"I had to leave before the doctor and her mother returned. The doctor said he'd suffered a mild heart attack. Who knows what that means? They were intending to run further tests on him. Time will tell, I suppose."

"At least he's in the right place if anything else happens to him."

"That's true. I'll speak with you later."

She ran up the stairs and bumped into DCI Blake at the top. "Sorry, sir. I'm in a rush."

"I can see that. Why?"

She gave him a brief rundown of what had happened in the last hour.

"Shit! Is her father going to be all right?"

"We won't know, not yet. They're carrying out further tests on him." She was already sick to the back teeth of repeating the same information.

"Okay, let me know how that goes, will you? Wish her father well when you speak with Carla again."

"I will. Thank you, sir. I need to crack on now."

"Of course. The last thing I want to do is hold you up, Inspector. You know where I am if you need me."

"I do. Thanks, sir."

Sara entered the incident room and brought the rest of the team up to date with the news. Then she wandered over to Carla's desk and examined the tabs she had open. "Craig, come here, please."

Craig joined her. "Yes, Boss."

"Take a seat. I want you to see what else you can find out about this committee, good and bad. I'm sensing this is where the investigation is going to lead us. The more we're up to speed on what happened decades ago, the better equipped we'll be going forward."

"Leave it with me. I'll see what I can find out."

She weaved her way through the desks towards Jill. "Have you found anything about the woman I spoke to earlier? Amanda Keller?"

"I've searched for any Amanda Kellers in the area but I've yet to find one. So, either she doesn't live in Hereford now or..."

"She gave me a false name," Sara finished off for her.

"Exactly."

"Bummer, okay. Keep searching, Jill."

Sara could sense everyone's mounting frustration. She made each team member a coffee and took hers through to the office. She stopped to take in the view; sometimes, it helped bring some semblance of order to her muddled mind. That wasn't the case this time. She sat behind her desk, sipped her drink, and, needing to hear her father's voice, she rang him. "Hi, it's Sara. How are you, Dad?"

"This is a surprise, you calling me during the day, sweetheart. Is everything all right?"

"Yes. I just needed to hear your voice. What are you up to?"

"Well, as it happens, Margaret is here with me. We're planning an itinerary for another holiday in the campervan. You don't mind, do you?"

"Mind? Why should I? Bloody hell, you're entitled to live your life the way you want to live it. Fair play to you. Where are you thinking of going?"

"Scotland. The Highlands to be precise. Actually, we're looking at doing the North Coast five hundred route. It was something your mother and I spoke about going on during our retirement. Unfortunately, we never got around to doing it. It was Margaret's suggestion, wasn't it, love?"

Tears filled her eyes. Finding Margaret at his age had turned out to be a blessing in disguise. She heard Margaret agree in the background, and then there was the sound of a kiss.

"Get a room, you two," she said, forgetting who she was talking to.

"I beg your pardon," her father admonished. "We'll do no such thing."

"Sorry, Dad. It was a joke."

"Not a very good one, daughter of mine. As I was saying, we're probably going to be away for about a month, if that's all right with you."

Sara laughed. "Why are you asking for my permission? You're both retired with no ties, so go for it. If anything, I'm envious of the freedom you have to be able to go away at the drop of a hat."

"Your time will come in the future. You sound a bit down. Is everything okay? Is Mark all right?"

"Yes, he's fine. Carla's father was rushed to hospital earlier with a suspected heart attack. The doctor thinks it was a mild one, and they're running further tests on him."

"Sorry to hear that. Pass on my best wishes to him. So that's behind your call, making sure I haven't got any health issues that I'm keeping under wraps, eh?"

"Not at all. I check in when I can. I'll leave you to work on your adventure. I'll speak to you both soon."

"All right. I'm always here if you need to chat, Sara."

"I know. I love you, Dad. Say hi to Margaret for me."

"I will. Take care. Love you."

"Ditto." She ended the call and sat back in her chair, feeling grateful that her father had someone special in his life to share his adventures with, instead of sitting at home, grieving the loss of her mother. She knew her mother would be watching over them, sending her blessing.

*May they have plenty more adventures ahead of them. That's what life is all about, taking the opportunities presented to you.*

———————

## 7

"It's okay. I'll chase that up when I'm back in the office. Thanks for letting me know, Simon. I'll be in touch soon."

Oliver Grant hung up and stretched his arms over his head. A knock sounded on his office door. "Come in."

The electrician, who was rewiring the old manor house he'd just bought, poked his head into the room. "I wanted to warn you that the power will be going off in half an hour."

"How long will it be off for?"

"A couple of hours. Sorry for the inconvenience. Needs must, so there's no way around it."

"Don't worry. Do what you need to do. I'll take Jackson for a walk. It'll make a change for him. We need to explore what the area has to offer in respect of dog-walking routes. This'll be our opportunity to do that. I'll get out of your hair soon, I promise."

"No rush. I wanted to give you the heads-up rather than just switch it off like most electricians would."

"That's good of you. Can I get you a drink before I go?"

"I never say no to a coffee. Thanks." The electrician got back to work.

Oliver tidied up his desk, put the more important documents he was working on in his top drawer and locked it. "Come on, Jackson, today is your lucky day, pal."

He prepared the coffee and delivered it to Matt, the electrician, before he put on his wellies, flat cap and jacket, then set off.

All the stresses of the day fell away as he strolled up the driveway with his dog. He'd had two strenuous weeks of negotiation with one of his top clients and was in dire need of a break. His girlfriend, Lucy, was eager to take off for the Maldives, but he wasn't the type to lie around on a beach all day. In fact, nothing could be more boring in his eyes. He'd rather climb some of the fells up in the Lake District with Jackson by his side. He patted his dog's head. "You'd love that, wouldn't you, boy?"

Jackson whimpered in response. Oliver took a right turn at the bottom of his long drive and was soon in the woodland that he could see from his office window. He let Jackson off the lead and threw a stick for him to chase. Jackson barked excitedly and returned moments later, dropping the stick in front of him, ready for round two. They walked further into the woods. Oliver scanned the area and beamed.

"How wonderful to have all this just a stone's throw, or should I say, a stick's throw, from the house. How lucky are we, Jackson?"

The dog barked then bounced up and down on all four paws until Oliver launched the stick again.

"I can't believe how much energy you have."

The game lasted over half an hour until Jackson dropped the stick and fell into stride beside him. "Good boy. Let's walk and recover for a few minutes. I wonder what route we should take. You choose. Shall we go left or right here?"

Jackson took the right path at the fork ahead of them, and Oliver soon realised it led upwards. The incline was gentle at first, but before long, he found his heart rate accelerating as the path grew steeper. After his earlier exertions, Jackson was struggling, too.

"Come on, boy, let's call it a day now. I think we'll need to explore this area more in the future. Maybe go a little further each time until we've built up our fitness levels."

They turned and walked back down, retracing their steps carefully as the ground moved beneath their feet in certain areas. They came to the crossroads again, and Oliver took the other path at the fork, intrigued to see what they might find there. The path wound its way through the tree trunks. He pricked up an ear. *Is that water I can hear up ahead?*

He found out what the source of the noise was when the area opened up in front of him. "Wow, this place is stunning."

Jackson bounced beside him, eager to dip his toes in the water.

"Go on then, don't go in too deep. The water seems fast-flowing here." He glanced to his left and saw a small waterfall. "What a magnificent find this is. Be careful, Jackson."

Oliver sat on a huge boulder close to the river's edge and admired his surroundings while keeping one eye on Jackson. His dog splashed around, fetching stones from the river and placing them on the grass at his feet, hoping that he would begin a game of fetch again.

"You're incorrigible. You should be knackered, on your knees by now, but look at you, always eager for more."

He hurled the stone, and it plopped into the water. He cringed, sensing he'd thrown it too far out. The next second, he was on his feet, chasing Jackson, who had been swept away by the current.

"Jackson, hold on. I'm coming, boy."

He noticed the panic rising in the dog's eyes. He tried to run. There was a bend up ahead. There was nothing else he could do but get into the river with his four-legged companion to rescue him. He tried, but the strength of the water swept him off his feet. He clung to a tree root on the bank and pulled himself ashore. By this time, Jackson was out of sight. Acid seared Oliver's throat. He sprinted alongside the river until the grass verge ran out, then shouted for his dog.

"Jackson. I'll meet you further down the river. Hang in there. Get to the side, if you can."

Not knowing the area well enough, he had no idea what the layout was like up ahead. It didn't matter; all he could think about was saving his dog. There was no way he'd give up on him without even trying. His second wind kicked in. He set off, hopping over the jagged riverbank ahead. He'd lost sight of his dog long ago. Frantic, he upped his pace and turned his ankle as he rounded the next bend. Relief filled him when he saw Jackson pulling himself out of the river up ahead.

"That was a stroke of luck, wasn't it?"

He spun around to face the man who had whispered in his ear. "You? What are you doing here?"

"I fancied a stroll and stumbled across you and your dog in need of rescuing, so I thought I'd lend you a hand."

"I don't need a hand. My dog is safe now. You have work to do. I thought you were going to install the new wiring in the house while we were out."

"That's what I wanted you to believe. You see, I had it all planned. I was going to follow you and chase you through the woods, but then all this happened. It's given me such a thrill watching you rescue your dog. Glad he's safe now. I wonder if he's going to react the same way when you're fearing for your life in the river."

"What? Are you insane?"

"Quite possibly. Get in there. Don't bother stripping off either. The weight of your clothes will help pull you under. That'll save me the job of getting my hands dirty again."

"What are you talking about?"

"Ah, you'll find out soon. Now, get closer to the water."

Oliver's eyes darted from the river back to the man who had been working in his house all week. "What are you going to do to me?"

In the distance, Jackson was leaping around, excited to have survived his traumatic trip down the river.

"I've told you what to do; stop wasting my time and do it!"

Oliver peered over his shoulder and took a step backwards.

"Fucking get on with it. What did I just tell you? Stop wasting my valuable time."

Another dog barked in the distance, and Jackson ran off to investigate the noise, leaving them alone.

"Don't even think about crying out for help. I'm warning you, things will end badly for you if you go against me."

"If I step into the river, I might never make it out alive, and you don't think that's going to end badly for me?" Oliver opened his mouth, ready to attract the attention of the dog owner, but the man he knew as Matt produced a knife from his sleeve and shook his head slowly.

"I wouldn't if I were you. Now, are you going to get in the river, or shall I do the deed here? The choice is yours."

"But... I can't swim," Oliver said the first words that came into his head.

"What kind of twat do you take me for? I've been in your home all week. You've got several photos around the house of yourself as a child, swimming in pools and at the beach with your parents."

"No. Those photos are of my nephew. You have to believe me. I can't swim."

"Bollocks. All the photos have your name and age on the back. Get in! This is your final chance."

Oliver took a step back as the man tentatively moved towards him, the knife raised and pure hatred evident in his eyes.

"Please, I'm begging you not to do this. If this is about money, I can give you a bonus for the work you've carried out for me this week. I've been delighted with what you've done so far. Let me transfer some money now." He withdrew his phone from his pocket.

Matt swiped it out of his grasp. "I won't tell you again. Do it! Get in the water. Now!"

"But my dog will be back soon. He'll panic if he sees me in the water."

"Jesus Christ, how many more times do I have to say it? I don't give a toss about your dog. You've got three seconds. One, two, three."

Oliver raised his hands as the man advanced quickly towards him. The movement was swift. He didn't realise what was happening until he felt blood dripping from the gash in his throat. He gripped his neck and then looked down at his bloody hands. He stumbled backwards. The man pushed him in the chest. The force of the water knocked him off his feet. He tried to shout for help, but the words failed to leave his lips. He was drifting, not only down the river, but also into unconsciousness.

*Help me, please!*

# 8

Sara called the usual team meeting the following morning, her head still spinning from what had happened the previous day with Carla's father. She'd rung her partner first thing to see if there was any news about her father. Carla had told her he was stable and that they intended to run more tests on him over the next couple of days to determine whether he'd need a stent, a pacemaker, or possibly even a heart bypass.

Sara was pleased that her partner had joined them. "Okay, you all know that Carla's father has a connection to this case, although that's not the reason he's in hospital. Carla rang him to ask about his involvement in the council committee that the two victims were connected to, and he suffered a minor heart attack. The news on that front is better than expected. I've placed an officer outside his room, just in case the killer gets wind that he's in hospital. Jill, any luck tracing the woman who contacted us after the press conference aired?"

"Still can't find anyone of that name, boss. I'm flummoxed as to what to do next."

"Could she be using her maiden name?" Carla suggested.

"It's worth a check. I'll go through the birth, death and marriage records, see if anything shows up there and get back to you."

"Thanks, Jill. That's a good shout, Carla." Sara smiled, appreciative of Carla's input to the meeting. "What I think we need to do is find a list of the people who were on that committee. I know it was twenty years ago. It's also important for us to see if there were any negative articles regarding the committee back in the day. So, let's get digging, folks. Work smarter not harder. I need you to think outside the box on this one."

"I think I can help with the list," Carla said, "but it would mean visiting my father and putting him under unnecessary pressure."

"No, we'll do it from our end. Let your father rest and recover. How is your mum holding up?"

"Mum is Mum. She's one of the strongest women I know. Her reaction to the news yesterday will have knocked her off course momentarily, but I'm betting she'll be firmly back on it today. She will be bossing the nursing staff around and ensuring Dad's every need is catered for. She slept there last night, in the chair beside him. The staff offered her a makeshift bed they keep for families, but she refused to leave his side."

"She's amazing. I hope her determination doesn't prove to be detrimental to her own health, though."

"Me, too. I'm going to keep an eye on her when I'm not here, trying to find the frigging killer. Why now? Why twenty years later?"

"That's what we need to find out."

Two hours later and things were looking up for the investigation. Carla found something buried in the archives that related to the committee's decision to knock down a housing estate to pave the way for a retail park on the edge of town.

"Interesting. Let's try to find out how many homes we're talking about here and what the consequences were. Do you know where it is?" Sara asked.

"Yes, I think I know. I need to check the facts out before I commit to anything."

"Always wise. Any news on the other members of this committee?"

"I've got an Oliver Grant here. I searched for his name, and it transpires that he's a local businessman. He's well thought of in the area. It might be worth calling him or going out to see him for a quick chat."

"Yes, I was thinking the same thing. Anyone else?"

"I have several more names. The first two I checked were already dead. They were in their sixties at the time the decision was made."

"Okay. Let's put that aside for now. Fancy going out to Grant's home? Unless he has an office in the city. If so, we can call there to see him."

"Let me see," Carla said. "Give me ten minutes to do the necessary digging."

AFTER FIVE MINUTES, Carla had all the information they needed to hand, and they drove to Grant's swanky office on the edge of the city centre. The receptionist approached the desk with a smile spreading across her ruby-red lips. Her makeup was over the top, probably better suited to nighttime than for wearing during the day.

Sara produced her ID. "We're here to see Oliver Grant. Is he available?"

"Ah, no. He's been working from home all week as he has the builders in."

"Okay. We'll visit him there."

"Do you have his address?"

Sara nodded. "We have it. Thanks."

"I'll give him a call and tell him to expect you."

Sara didn't try to dissuade her; she didn't see the point. Once they were outside the building, she said, "Let's hope he's still there when we show up."

"Unless he has something to hide, there's no reason why he should do a runner, is there?"

"Who knows with these business types? We didn't tell her why we needed to chat with him."

"That's true. It's about a fifteen-minute drive from here."

THEY DREW into the long drive, having found the gates open.

"Wow, this place is impressive. He must be doing well with his business."

"Maybe he took a few backhanders during the pandemic," Carla said, disgruntled.

"You crack me up. Not every businessman is bent, you know. Some make it big through sheer hard work and determination."

Carla faced her and raised an eyebrow as Sara drew to a halt outside the front door. "Really? Someone this wealthy?"

"God, I'd say you were far too young to be such a cynic."

"And I'd say you were talking out of your arse. Look at all the stories still coming out about the pals of those in the Tories who dished out PPE contracts. People who didn't have a clue about supplying the equipment, let alone manufacturing it."

"All right. Hey, you're going to need to calm down a bit before we go inside."

Carla sighed. "Sorry. I'm worried about my dad."

"I know you are, but being angry isn't going to help him, is it?"

"Okay. I've already apologised. I refuse to do it again."

Sara rolled her eyes. "Would you rather stay in the car and let me handle this?"

"No. I'll be fine. Let's see what the fucker has to say." Carla pulled the handle and went to get out of the car. "What's wrong? I thought you were keen to get in there."

"I am. But you're going to have to ditch the attitude first."

Carla flopped her head back. "I'm fine. If you'd rather I stay here, it suits me."

"I would. I'll see if he's in, first."

"He should be. He's got the builders in, remember? Although, I can't see any other vehicles here apart from the Merc with the personalised plate, which must be his."

"Good point." Sara exited the vehicle and walked up the five steps to the entrance. She rang the bell that echoed around the inside, and turned to survey the view. She loved that there was a forest opposite the house, and on either side of it were fields leading to rolling hills in the distance. After waiting a few minutes, she rang the bell again. Still no answer. She tried the knob on the front door, and it opened. She beckoned Carla to join her.

Carla reluctantly got out of the car and stomped up the steps. "What's going on?"

"That's what I'd like to find out. We need to check it out together. I should have booked out a Taser, but I didn't think it would be necessary."

"And now you do?"

"I'm not sure. Why would the owner of a house this size leave the front door open?"

"There's only one way to find out."

Sara pushed open the door. There was some equipment in the hallway and a white sheet covering the marble floor. "Why aren't the builders here?"

Carla crossed the hallway and examined the equipment. "It's junction boxes. Everything you'd need to rewire a place this size, but no tradesman's tools. That's strange."

"Maybe the builder was waiting for the electrician to show up. Perhaps he's been delayed and is working on another job at the moment."

Carla shook her head. "Maybe, but something doesn't feel right. Damn, I'm turning into you."

Sara laughed. "That'll be the day. Let's search each room and see what we can find. It's strange that there are no workmen on site."

"Hmm..."

Sara checked the rooms on the left, while Carla checked the ones on the right.

"I've found his office," Carla said.

She walked inside, and Sara joined her.

Carla wiggled the mouse on the desk. "The screen had switched to sleep mode. He can't be far."

Sara strained her ear. "Ssh... I can hear sirens approaching." She rushed to the front door, with Carla close behind her.

Two patrol cars screeched to a halt outside the woodland opposite. Sara's stomach muscles tightened. She sensed something was amiss and was eager to find out what was going on. "I'll be right back."

"Hey, I'm coming with you. I have no intention of staying here by myself."

They bolted up the drive to the uniformed officers who had assembled.

"What's going on?" she asked one of the officers she knew.

"Hello, ma'am. We've received a call from a member of the public saying that a body has been found down by the river."

"What? Male or female?"

"Male. There's a dog sitting by his side. The couple who discovered him couldn't get near to check if he was all right. They think he's dead. We're going to have to deal with the dog first, if you get what I mean."

Sara raised a finger. "Don't harm it. There's no need for you to do that. Put a call in for a dog handler to come down here."

"Very well, ma'am. I'll do that now." The officer placed the call to the station as he led the group through the woods down to the river.

In the far distance, Sara could hear the frantic barking of the dog.

The group raced towards the noise and found a middle-aged couple with a red setter on a lead, standing fifty feet away from the river. The barking dog was standing close to a man who was lying on the bank, his legs still in the water.

"This doesn't look good, does it?" Carla said.

"Nope. I agree. Do you want to talk to them? They seem really upset, which is totally understandable. Get their details and the account of what they found and send them on their way. We can sort out a statement later. It might calm the defensive dog down if the couple and their dog left."

"I agree. I'll have a word with them."

"Does anyone here have a dog?" Sara asked the group of officers.

"I used to. We lost him a few years ago. Not fair having a dog if we're at work all day, ma'am."

"I agree. I own a cat for that very reason. Do you want to attempt to calm the dog down? My partner is going to get the other couple and their dog away from the area ASAP. Be ready to make a move once they get on their way."

The officer wiped his palms on his trousers and glanced over at the dog, who seemed hoarse. Sara assumed it must have been barking for a while. Poor thing. It was doing an excellent job of protecting its owner, but now they needed it to stand down and allow them to get closer.

Carla walked past with the couple and their dog. Sara said hello to them.

The barking dog seemed a little more at ease now that the other dog was leaving. Sara felt relieved and tried to approach the animal with the other officer. Its hackles immediately rose again, so they backed away. The officer spoke gently to the dog and took a few steps forward. The dog looked back at its owner. It seemed confused, and Sara feared for their safety if they got any closer.

"I think we should wait for the K9 officer to arrive. They'll know how to proceed."

They both backed away, and the dog seemed to calm down again. It walked back to his owner, licked his face, then sat and stared at Sara and the other officers. Her heart went out to the faithful hound.

Carla joined her a few minutes later. "The couple found him like this. They rang nine-nine-nine right away. They haven't been able to assess the man's condition because of the dog. He looks dead to me."

"Well, he hasn't moved since we arrived. He's too far away to see if he has any injuries."

"Let me see if my camera can pick anything up." Carla removed her mobile and zoomed in. She showed Sara the image on the screen.

"Clever dick. Is that an injury to his throat?"

"Yep. I can't see him picking that up just from being in the water."

"So, his throat was deliberately cut, and then he was thrown in? What the fuck? How did the attacker get close to him, considering how the dog is acting right now?"

"I don't know. It's hard to tell. Maybe the dog was playing fetch in the water and someone came along and sliced the man's throat while the dog was distracted."

"Possibly. Ah, here we are. Another officer has arrived; he must be from the K9 team."

"What's going on?" the officer asked.

Sara told him what had happened and asked for his assistance.

He patted the bag attached to his belt. "I've got this covered. I always have treats to hand in case of emergencies. We often deal with aggressive dogs during raids. A piece of chicken on hand can work wonders. Watch and learn, folks."

The K9 officer spoke to the dog, which was now back on its feet in full attack mode. The officer got closer and started throwing the chicken ahead of it. The dog showed some interest in the treats and allowed him to get closer. He removed a lead from around his neck, placed a handful of chicken in front of the dog, and once it had finished its snack, he slipped the lead around its neck and walked away with it.

Sara, Carla and the rest of the officers ran to the riverbank. The blood surrounding the man was enough to confirm he was dead.

"Do you want me to call Lorraine?" Carla asked.

"You might as well. I don't think there's any way back for him." Sara observed the victim from different angles whilst listening to Carla as she spoke to Lorraine.

The dog had relaxed and was whimpering next to the K9 officer, probably sensing that nothing further could be done for its master.

Sara slipped on a pair of gloves and got down on her haunches. She searched the man's pockets and found his wallet. "Ah, looks like we're in luck." She removed his driving licence and swore under her breath.

"Not good news, I take it?"

"You could say that. He's Oliver Grant."

"Holy shit! So, he was out here on a walk with the dog. That's why his house was unlocked."

Sara removed an evidence bag from her pocket and dropped the wallet into it. She rubbed her chin with her hand. "Who killed him? Why choose this area? Was it one of the builders?"

"It seems strange that there were no workmen at the house when we arrived," Carla added.

"That's got to be our first step. Find out who was carrying out the renovation work. Ring the station and get Jill to check with his office to see if they know. Also, ask the team to check if he was asking for any recommendations for tradesmen on his social media accounts. We can't ask the neighbours because he doesn't have any. Was he lured to this location on purpose? Or did someone follow him down here from the house? What did the couple who found him have to say?"

"Nothing much. They saw him lying there and called out to him. When they got no response, they rang nine-nine-nine. It's got to be the same killer, hasn't it?"

Sara shrugged and glanced over at the man's dog. "Probably. It would be too much of a coincidence otherwise. Wait..." She faced Carla. "A house like that would have security cameras, wouldn't it?"

Carla raised her eyebrows and pointed her finger. "He'd be foolish not to. Shall we go back and take a look?"

"Let's leave it for now. We can check it out after Lorraine and the team get here. Now, I think we should make use of the extra manpower at our disposal and conduct a thorough search of the area."

"Okay. What should we be searching for? Anything in particular?"

"I can't see a phone nearby. I find it hard to believe that an entrepreneur would leave their phone at home."

"I'm with you. Yes, you're right. I'll get them to fan out and examine the route back through the woods."

"Thanks. While you do that, I'll have a word with the K9 officer."

They separated. Sara walked towards the officer, who was crouching next to the dog and petting it. The poor dog didn't react to her arrival.

"We've identified the man. What we're unsure of is if anyone else lives at the residence. Is there any way we can look after the dog for the next twenty-four hours or so? I'd hate to put him in a kennel; it seems like he's been through enough already."

"I can take him back to base and see if we can accommodate him for a while. If not, I'll take him home with me."

"That's kind of you."

The officer shrugged. "He trusts me. He might revert to being aggressive if I turn him over to someone else. He's a good lad. All he was doing was protecting his master."

"He's a devoted dog. It's a shame it has ended this way for them both. I'll give you my card and get my team to do the necessary research for next of kin et cetera, if you can give me a call at around five this evening."

"I'll do that, ma'am. All right if we leave now?"

"Of course. We're going to be here a while yet. Thanks for your assistance."

"You're welcome. I'll be in touch later."

Sara watched the officer walk away with the dog on a relaxed lead. He turned to look at his master now and again en route back to the officer's car.

Sara took a gamble and rang the station. "Jill, I know I'm asking a lot of you guys back there, but any news for me?"

"I rang his office, but they couldn't tell me who he had employed. So, we're none the wiser."

"Okay, not to worry. As soon as the pathologist arrives, Carla and I are going to trek back to the house to see if there are any cameras on site. Get someone else to go through the SM accounts. I'd like you to start on the background checks for Grant, including his financials, and I'm going to need to know who, if anyone, he shares his home with. It is a stunning manor house, by the way, with no nearby neighbours and set in an idyllic location."

"Hang on, I'd already started some brief research. He's recently gone through a divorce with his wife, Tania Grant, who lives in Breinton, at seven Dormer Road. I also spotted an article in the local paper from two weeks ago stating that he was now seeing a socialite nearly half his age, Lucy Holden."

"Wow, well done, you. And does she live at the residence?"

"I haven't found any proof of that yet. I'll keep searching and get back to you. No doubt we'll find the information on social media."

"Okay, I'll leave it with you. We'll be back when we can. Give me a call with any information you gather."

"You can count on it, boss. Take care."

Sara ended the call and walked across the field to where Carla had just finished issuing orders to the other officers. "We should join in. I reckon he came from further up the river and was washed up on the bank as it slowed on the bend."

"Maybe the dog rescued him."

Sara shrugged. They walked back towards the forest, scanning the ground within a few feet of them. The sun glinted on something ahead, and Sara upped her pace to see what it was. She pulled on a pair of gloves and bent to pick up the mobile.

"I've found it."

Carla rushed to join her. "Well, at least this should give us a few answers."

"Let's hope so." Sara spotted movement out of the corner of her eye and released a relieved sigh. "It's Lorraine and her team. We'll make her aware of what has happened and then do what is necessary back at the house."

Lorraine seemed grumpy giving orders to her team, so Sara trod carefully. "Hi, thanks for coming, Lorraine. Is everything all right?"

"What do you think? If you're here, this can only mean one thing: the crimes are linked, am I right?"

"Give that woman a Gold Blue Peter Badge for being such a superstar." Sara did her best to prevent the situation escalating.

"Cut the crap. What do we know about the victim?"

"What we've discovered during the investigation so far is that the killings have something to do with a committee that disbanded around twenty years ago." Sara glanced at Carla, and she nodded. "We suspect Carla's father was part of that committee."

That gained the pathologist's attention. "Was he now? Has anything happened to him? What does he have to say about all of this?"

"I tried to get what information I could out of him over the phone. He collapsed, and I had to rush over to the house," Carla explained.

"Oh no, I hope he's all right," Lorraine said, shocked.

"He had a minor heart attack and is in hospital. They're carrying out extra tests. Sorry, I'm going on. What I'm trying to say is that I won't be able to talk about the investigation, not without upsetting him or causing further damage."

"Shit! Sorry to hear that. I can totally understand your dilemma. What about looking through the archives?"

"The team is doing that now," Sara interjected. "We'd tracked down the victim and were at his house when the patrol cars showed up. We asked what was going on, and they told us that a body had been found. We had no indication that the body would turn out to be the man we were hoping to see."

"Really? Wow, okay. What are you saying? That someone got wind of you coming out here and bumped him off before you arrived?"

"No, that would imply that we have a mole on our team, and I can categorically shoot that notion down in flames. I'm putting it down to coincidence. We stopped by Grant's office and were told that he was working from home this week because his house was being renovated. When we got there, the front door was unlocked and there was electrical equipment in the hallway but no sign of any tradesmen on site."

"Interesting. Who else lives at the property?" Lorraine asked, her attention drawn downriver.

"He's recently got divorced, but we believe he's now seeing a woman half his age. We're not sure if she's moved in or not. That's next on our agenda: to go back to the house and give it a thorough search."

"Well, what are you waiting for? I think we'll be here for hours." Lorraine peered at the sky. "Providing the weather is kind to us. No dark clouds overhead as yet. Right, I must crack on."

"Yes, we're going to do the same. Before we go, the victim had a dog with him that was super protective of its owner. We had to call a K9 expert out to handle it. He's removed it from the scene. The victim was found downriver, but his mobile was discovered here."

Lorraine placed a thumb and forefinger around her chin. "Someone attacked him here and threw him into the river. The current carried him away. Maybe the dog was the one who rescued him and pulled him out of the water."

"We assumed the same. So, what I'm trying to say is that there are two areas for you and your team to work on out here, not just the one."

Lorraine clicked her fingers. "Put a couple of markers in this area before we move on."

"Yes, boss. Any reason?"

Lorraine tutted. "It's possible the victim might have been attacked here and then thrown in the river."

"Right you are. Doing it now." The tech dipped his hand into his bag and removed several yellow, tent-shaped, numbered markers, which he placed on the ground.

"We'll show you where the body is," Sara said.

They chatted as they walked back to where the victim was lying.

"You're going to need to up your game on this one, Sara, to prevent any other deaths occurring," Lorraine pointed out.

"You reckon? What do you think we're trying to do? We spent a few hours at the hospital with Carla's father, not knowing how serious his condition was, then we came here to see the victim; however, we arrived too late." Her voice rose, letting Lorraine know how frustrated she was without having to spell it out for her.

Lorraine raised her hands. "All right. I was only giving you some advice."

"Well, don't. You do your job, and I'll do mine. Now, do you need us to hang around any longer, or can we get on with the investigation?"

Lorraine narrowed her eyes and wagged her finger. "Don't pull that attitude with me, Sara, otherwise you and I are going to fall out, you hear me?"

Sara sighed and laid a hand on her friend's arm. "Sorry, I didn't mean to take out my foul mood on you. Give me a call later, once you've performed the PM, if you wouldn't mind."

Lorraine smiled. "Only if you promise to be in a better mood by then."

Sara and Carla headed back to the car.

Sara called over her shoulder, "I can't promise that, but I'll do my best."

BACK AT THE HOUSE, they snapped on another pair of gloves and began their search. Outside, Carla had spotted two neat cameras that were slotted into a couple of nooks above the front door.

"Good spot. I doubt if many people would know they were there."

"The question is, would the killer see them?"

"If he's an electrician, I'm going to take a punt that he would. We need to find the security equipment. Again, I'm going to take a gamble and suggest it might be in Grant's office."

They wandered through the extensive hallway to his office. The first thing Sara noticed was how tidy it was. It hadn't been ransacked, which would have indicated that someone was searching for something.

There was a small desk behind the main one. On it was a screen and what appeared to be some form of recording equipment. Sara switched on the screen and pressed the Play button. The screen split into four. One view was of the front door, the second of the back door, the third was in the kitchen, and the fourth showed the view of the hallway.

"I think we're in luck. If the electrician was the one who put all that equipment there, then the camera should have caught his movements in the hallway, as well as entering the house via the front door, if that's the way he came in. I'm excited to see the results."

"I'd tamp down that excitement if I were you. The killer might have taken the recent footage with him before he left the premises."

"There's only one way to find out." Sara fiddled with the equipment, but nothing came up on the screen. She pressed the Eject button and found the tray empty. "Shit! You did warn me."

A scream sounded behind them, scaring the crap out of them. Sara turned to see a blonde standing in the doorway. She'd removed a pepper spray from her small handbag and was rushing towards them.

Sara withdrew her ID from her jacket pocket. "Stop right there. We're the police. Fire that, and I'll have you for assaulting a police officer."

The woman paused mid-step. Her brow furrowed in confusion. "The police? What are you doing in my house?"

"Your house? Oh, sorry, I thought the property belonged to Mr Grant."

"I share it with him; therefore, it's my property as well. Don't get smart with me. I asked you a question. What are you doing here?" She replaced the spray in her handbag and continued to walk towards them.

"Can you tell me your name?"

"Lucy Holden. What's yours? And why are you evading my question?"

"I'm not, not on purpose anyway. I'm DI Sara Ramsey, and this is my partner, DS Carla Jameson."

"Right. Now we've established that, what are you doing here in my home?"

"I have no problem telling you, but I think you should take a seat first."

She crossed her arms and stuck out her right hip in defiance. "I'm fine as I am. Now tell me. That is, unless you want me to report you for breaking in."

"We didn't. The front door was open when we arrived."

Her lip curled, and she looked them both up and down with contempt. "I don't believe you."

Sara shrugged. "It wasn't open for discussion. I was merely stating facts."

"Whatever. Get on with it and then you can leave my house."

"Very well, if that's what you want. When was the last time you saw Oliver Grant?"

"Yesterday. I've been at my friend's house overnight. Why?"

"You were having renovations done, right?"

"Yes, you can see that from the state the hallway is in. Why? And by the way, I'm getting fed up with asking why at the end of every answer, just so you know."

"Can you tell us the name of the firm Mr Grant used?"

"No. *Why?* You're beginning to piss me off now." She unfolded her arms and stamped her foot. Then she moved to sit in the executive chair.

Sara inhaled a large breath and let it out slowly. She had a feeling about how the young woman would react once she shared the news of Grant's death. "It is with regret that I have to tell you that Oliver Grant's body was discovered down by the river earlier."

Lucy sat upright and stared at her. "Define body?"

"His dead body," Sara clarified.

"What the fuck are you talking about? Is this your frigging idea of a joke? It's gone April Fool's Day, so I know it can't be that. Have you arrested him?"

"No. I told you. His body was found by the river earlier by a couple of dog walkers."

She screamed, covered her eyes with her hands and rocked back and forth. "No. You're lying. This can't be true. I won't believe it until I see him for myself."

"Are his parents still alive?"

"No. They both died around five years ago. What's that got to do with anything?"

"As you weren't married to him, they would have been considered his next of kin."

"What? What does that matter? We were living together. Are you telling me I can't see him?"

"No. If you were classed as a couple, then yes, you'll be able to see him once the post-mortem has been carried out."

"A what?"

"A post-mortem. It's when the pathologist examines the body..."

"Bloody hell, I'm not thick. I know what it is. I thought they were only performed on a body when a suspicious death has occurred."

"That's correct. Oliver was murdered."

"And you're just telling me that now? Who the fuck do you think you are, lady? I'm his girlfriend. I have a right to know how he died and what you're doing about his murder."

"I'm sorry. I won't be able to tell you what the cause of death is until I receive the pathologist's report."

"That's utter bullshit. Where is he? I saw all the vehicles parked outside the gates. I wondered who they belonged to. Is that the pathologist and his team?"

"The pathologist is female. No, you won't be able to get close to the crime scene. It'll be taped off to members of the public."

"I'm not just any member of the public. I'm his girlfriend, for fuck's sake. Why do you persist in disrespecting me?"

"I'm not. I'm sorry if you believe that. All I'm doing is following the correct procedures for when a body has been found."

"I have a right to see him. I'm going down there. He's obviously still there."

"They won't allow you to get close to him, whether you're his girl-friend or not. I'm truly sorry for your loss."

"Why? Why has someone killed him? Do you know?" Lucy asked, a little calmer now.

How long that would last, Sara didn't know.

"We believe it's to do with an ongoing investigation. We came out here to talk with Oliver. We found the door unlocked, and then the officers arrived. We enquired what they were doing here, and they told us that a body had been found down by the river. We went down there to see who it was and found Oliver's wallet on him, confirming his ID."

She shook her head. "But why was he killed? What sort of investigation have you been running? I don't understand any of this. We were happy together, and now, all that has gone. Why would someone want to kill him?"

"As I said, we have every reason to suspect it's linked to something that happened over twenty years ago."

Lucy stared at her. "Is that it? Can't you tell me anything else?"

"Not really, not yet. My team is working hard to uncover the details. It's proving difficult at this time, which is why we came to see Oliver and ask what he could tell us about it."

"You must have something more than that. What are you keeping from me?"

"Nothing, not intentionally. This week, two other men have been killed, and our investigation suggests there could be a connection between the victims."

"What connection? And what does this have to do with Oliver?"

"All three men were involved in a committee twenty years ago. Something loosely to do with the council. As I said, that's as much as we know right now. We came here to interview Oliver about what went on back in the day but arrived too late. The killer got here first."

Lucy shook her head in disbelief. "Hang on, why were you asking about the electrician? Do you think he did this?"

"Yes, there's a distinct possibility. That's why we were in here looking at the security system. There were no workmen here when we arrived. We might be doing him an injustice. He could have just gone to pick up some supplies, and we believe it might be why Oliver left the door unlocked when he took his dog for a walk."

"My God, I didn't even notice that Jackson was missing." Lucy leapt out of the chair and ran towards the door.

"Please, don't worry about him. Jackson was protecting Oliver. We had to call a K9 officer in to calm him down. Jackson has been taken to the station. He wasn't harmed, I promise."

"Thank God. He's precious to both of us. I know Oliver has had him a few years, but I love him just as much as Oliver did." She collapsed against the wall and placed her hands on her thighs. "I can't believe he's gone. How can someone be so vile as to take another person's life? What gives them the right to do it?"

"It's hard to believe. We will get to the bottom of this, I promise you. I have to ask if Oliver has received any strange phone calls or visits lately, apart from the electrician?"

"I don't know. He runs, sorry, he ran, several successful businesses; he was always on the phone, day and night. It used to drive me nuts. To be honest, I tended to switch off most of the time. Can't you trace his calls? But wait, you said you thought it was the electrician. Has that changed now?"

"No, I'm simply covering all the bases just in case the electrician is innocent."

"I know this is going to sound selfish, but can you tell me what's going to happen to this place now that he's gone?"

Sara shrugged. "The honest answer is, I don't know. I suppose that will depend on whether his will was up to date or not. Wasn't he recently divorced from his wife?"

"Oh, shit! Yes, I don't know if he'd got around to changing his will. I think he had every intention of doing it, his solicitor advised him to, but his businesses have been mega busy lately, and I don't think he got around to it. Does that mean she'll get the house? And that I'll be kicked out?"

"I can't tell you that. The only one who would be able to advise you is his solicitor. You'll need to give him a call and see what he can tell you."

"Thanks. I know it sounds awful to ask, but I gave up my home to move in here."

"I don't suppose there will be any rush for you to move out. His estate will probably have to go through probate, which could take months to get sorted."

"I see. I wasn't aware of that. I'm sorry to ask."

"Don't be. Please, if there is anything about this electrician that you can remember, it would be a great help to our investigation."

She shrugged and sighed. "I can't. I barely noticed him. Yes, he worked here, but I have my own career. I'm a mobile beautician. I was at my friend's house yesterday, doing a few of her friends' nails, and as I was running late, she asked me to stay the night. I rang Oliver. He told me to have fun. I had another client this morning, hence the reason why I am only just getting home now. So, I really haven't been around that much while the electrician has been on site."

"It would be helpful if we knew what firm he worked for. Did Oliver have a diary?"

"It's on his phone. Have you found that?"

"Yes, we found it down by the river, a few hundred feet from where his body was discovered."

"What? That's strange, isn't it? He was glued to that phone."

"I had a suspicion that might be the case. We believe Oliver was attacked further upriver and that the killer probably tried to dispose of his body in the river. He was found on the riverbank. We suspect he was either washed ashore or that Jackson might have dived in to save him. The dog was wet when we found it. They both were."

"Oh God. He was devoted to Oliver. Can he come home?"

"I can arrange that. I'll call the officer now. He didn't leave that long ago." Sara left the room to call the station after realising she hadn't taken the officer's number. They patched her through to him. "Hi, it's DI Sara Ramsey. We met a little while ago."

"Yes, ma'am. Is everything okay?"

"Can you bring the dog to the house close to where you parked earlier? The owner's girlfriend is here, concerned about it. It's called Jackson by the way."

"No problem. I'll be with you shortly."

"Thanks. Sorry to mess you about."

"You haven't."

Sara ended the call and returned to the office. "He's on his way."

"Thank goodness. Jackson is such a sensitive soul. He'll be

confused by what's happened to Oliver. I can't wait to give him a cuddle."

"Is there anything else you can think of that we should know about?"

She shook her head again. "No, I don't think so."

"Very well. We're going to leave you to it then and get on with the investigation. The CD was missing from the recorder, but we've taken one that was lying on the desk. It might give us a lead as to who the electrician is. I hope that's all right?"

"Of course. Take whatever you need if you think it might help. I don't want to stand in your way of getting a result. I'm worried, though, about the electrician. What if he returns?"

"If he shows up again, which I doubt, especially if he's the person responsible, keep the doors locked and call the station ASAP. I'll leave you my card; ring me or dial nine-nine-nine and someone will come out immediately." She handed Lucy a card.

"Thank you. That'll give me some peace of mind."

"Looking at the gear littering the hallway, we couldn't see any tools there, so there's every chance he won't return."

"I hadn't noticed."

"Let's wait and see if he comes back. In the meantime, we'll be trying hard to find him. Hopefully, the recording will point us in the right direction. We'll show ourselves out. The officer should be here soon, and having Jackson back in the house should give you some comfort. Be wary of anyone else showing up."

"I will. I'll refuse to let anyone else in and use the chain on the door."

Sara and Carla left and walked back to the car.

"Well, that turned out better than I thought it was going to be," Sara said.

"Yep. I thought she was going to be the hysterical type. Although she started off that way, she calmed down considerably once she realised Grant was dead and nothing could change that fact. What next?" Carla asked.

Sara chewed her lip and faced her. "We could really do with having a chat with your father, you know, to get to the bottom of this."

Carla tutted. "It's too soon, Sara. I know we need to interview him, but I can't allow that to happen, not until the doctors give us the all-clear."

"All right. Let's get back to the station, then."

## 9

They returned to the station to the news that the rest of the team, between them, had unearthed what might be the motive for the murders.

Jill ran through what they had discovered in the archives. "It was well hidden, plus the information I found is relatively sparse. In 2004, the council committee agreed to demolish a small housing estate in favour of creating a shopping complex."

"That's the one Carla had already picked up, isn't it? The one on the edge of the city?"

"No. This one is further out of town, towards Belmont."

Sara folded her arms and perched on the desk behind her while Carla made everyone a drink. "Go on. What else have you found?"

Carla handed round the coffees and said, "Hang on, if this electrician turns out to be the culprit, maybe he had something to do with the development of the complex. Maybe the council screwed him over, paid him less than he was expecting to receive from the job."

"Hmm... it's a possibility. Is there a way we can check who the contractors were that worked on the site, Jill?"

"I can certainly look into it, boss."

"But why now? Twenty years later?" Sara asked.

"Yeah, that's what we're going to need to dig deep to find out," Carla said.

"Can anyone tell me what happened to the people who lived in the properties where the complex was built?"

"As far as I can tell, the estate was council-owned, so presumably the council would have moved them to other accommodation."

"If there had been any available at the time. Judging by today's standards, I doubt if there were many options on offer."

"Yeah, I agree," Carla said. "Would it be worth knocking on a few doors in the area? If it's a close-knit community, maybe the residents of the houses opposite rallied around and helped their neighbours when the time came for them to move out."

Sara nodded and continued to think about the prospect. "That's not a bad shout. Let's have our drinks and then hit the road."

"Just us?" Carla asked, shocked. "We'll have to cover a pretty big area."

"No, we'll all go. Except you, Jill. Can you continue digging into the archives? Craig, see what you can find on the security disc first before we head off."

"I've had a quick gander, boss, and found this." He turned on the large TV on the wall using the remote control. On the camera outside the property, a white van arrived.

Sara stepped forward and took a closer look at the number plate. "That's got to be fake, hasn't it?"

"I think so. It doesn't seem right to me. The van also lacks signage on the side and back, which doesn't bode well for tracing it."

"Bugger. This killer knows exactly what to do to avoid being captured."

"Absolutely. There's more. The man jumps out of the van here."

The footage showed him leaving the vehicle. The driver wore a lumberjacket with a hooded sweatshirt underneath. He kept the hood up the whole time, even when the footage showed the man entering the hallway.

"Bugger, he never took it off? It must have been restrictive at times, surely?"

Craig nodded. "You'd think so. I've been watching him for a while, and I don't think it's a ruse. I believe he's a real electrician because he appeared to know his way around the circuit board and all the wiring as he was feeding it through the walls during the job."

"Okay, well, at least that's something to cling on to. You know what I'm going to request next? Let's make a list of all the electricians in the area. Hit Worcester as well and any other smaller towns in between and on the outskirts of Hereford. Actually, you continue to work on that throughout the day while we canvass the area."

"All right, boss. I don't mind either way."


NOT LONG AFTER, Sara and the rest of the team left the station and headed out towards Belmont.

Carla pointed ahead of them. "I know I'm stating the obvious here, but that's the complex they built. It's already looking tired after only twenty years. They don't build them to last these days, do they?"

"No, you can say that again. Right, so, we'll be cheeky and park in the supermarket car park and set off from there."

Their colleagues joined them as, together, they walked across the road towards the nearest housing estate.

"Christine, Marissa and Barry, why don't you take this side of the road, and Carla and I will start on the other? If you hear anything, give me a shout. You know what to ask. We specifically want to know where the previous residents moved to and how much they can tell us about what went on in the area, either before, during or after the erection of the complex. Don't bother talking to anyone who has lived here less than twenty years."

The team split up and began canvassing the tenants of the older-style properties.

Sara knocked on the first door, and it was opened by a young woman with a toddler attached to her hip. Sara held up her warrant card. "Hello, there. Sorry to trouble you. I'm with the West Mercia Police, based here in Hereford."

"And? Are you here to see me?"

"Oh no, sorry. We're canvassing the area in the hope that we might find some residents who have lived here just over twenty years."

The young woman laughed. "Well, you can count me out. I've only lived here for three years."

"Never mind. I don't suppose you'd happen to know any of your neighbours who might fit the bill, would you?"

"Gosh, let me think." She peered up the road and whispered, "The older residents have been dropping like flies lately. Old Mrs Purnell died only last week."

"That's sad. What about someone slightly younger, who is maybe in their fifties or sixties, perhaps?"

The little boy started playing with the buttons on her shirt. He quickly undid the top two to expose his mother's black lacy bra. "Oh my. He's a rascal, still eager to play with Mummy's boobs, given the chance."

Sara laughed. "I won't hold you up for too long."

"He's got to learn that Mummy's boobs aren't available twenty-four-seven. Let me think. There's Mrs Thatcher who lives halfway up the street on the other side of the road. I can't remember which number, though. Sorry."

"No problem. Thanks very much for your help. We'll check with your other neighbours. Good luck with what lies ahead of you."

The young mother rolled her eyes. "I'm going to need all the help I can get. I hope one of my neighbours can give you some information."

Sara waved and walked past Carla, who was talking to the neighbour next door. She knocked on the door, but it remained unanswered, so she tried the next house. Carla jogged past her to try the next house.

"Any luck?" Sara mouthed.

Carla shook her head.

The door opened, and a man in his thirties stood there, his hair wet and his top half bare. He had the skimpiest of towels slung around his waist. Sara struggled to keep her focus on his face. She explained why she was there and, while trying to prevent herself from blushing, asked, "Do you own the property?"

"No, I rent it."

"Ah, okay. Have you lived here long?"

"Six months."

"That's all I need to know. Sorry to have disturbed your shower."

"You didn't. You interrupted me getting dressed. I hope you enjoyed the view." He grinned and flicked the door shut in her face.

*Holy shit! What is wrong with me? I have a hunk of my own at home. I shouldn't be eyeing up other men with superb bodies, rippling muscles and... Jesus, get a grip.*

"Everything all right?" Carla asked as they passed each other on their way to the next two houses.

"The things you see during the day." She fanned her face with her hand, and Carla laughed.

They received mixed success from the houses they knocked on until they reached halfway up the road. Barry texted Sara to join him at one of the houses, which turned out to belong to Mrs Thatcher, the woman who had already been mentioned. Sara and Carla crossed the road to join the conversation.

"Boss, this is Mrs Thatcher. This is my senior officer, DI Ramsey."

"Hello, Mrs Thatcher. Have you lived here long?" Sara asked.

"Around forty years, I think. I've seen a lot of changes over the years. Not all of them good. Why do you ask?"

"We're conducting an investigation, and it's led us to this area." Watching her words, not wishing to upset the woman more than was necessary, Sara added, "We suspect the motive for the crime is linked to the construction of the shopping complex across the road."

"Ha, I'm not surprised. That horrendous site caused a lot of unrest in the area, not only when it was being built, but also when the news broke about what the council intended to do with the area. Heartless bastards, excuse my language. Dozens of people my age now were given a few months to move out of their homes. The corrupt council didn't give two hoots that some of those people had lived most of their lives in those properties. Folks didn't tend to move a lot in those days. A house was a home, not just bricks and mortar to some folks. The youngsters of today wouldn't understand that concept, would they?"

Sara smiled and removed her notebook from her pocket. "I'm inclined to agree with you. I wonder if you wouldn't mind giving us some names of the people who were worst affected by the disruption."

"Why don't you come in? I need to sit down. My legs aren't what they used to be. I'm on the damn waiting list for a hip operation. Lord knows when that is likely to be. I've been on it eight months now."

"Barry, why don't you and the rest of the team continue where we left off and see if anything else comes to light?" Sara asked.

Then she and Carla entered the house behind Mrs Thatcher. She shuffled through the dark hallway and into a lounge that was tidy but very dated.

"Do you have any family, Mrs Thatcher?"

"A son who can't be bothered with me most of the time. He only shows up when he needs money out of me. Owes me bloody thousands, he does. Every time he leaves, I give myself a good talking-to for being such an idiot, but I still do the same the next time he comes knocking."

"Sorry to hear that. Do you have any other children?"

Her face lit up. "Yes, I have my Catherine, the light of my life. She lives on the other side of the world, in Australia. We FaceTime each other every week. She includes me in all their parties. I'm there, in the background, joining in. I think that's what gets under Dennis' skin most of the time. That's my selfish, ungrateful son. I really must learn to say no to him."

Sara sensed there was more to the story than the old lady was letting on. "Is there a reason why you don't say no?"

"He's not been the same since I lost Bill, my husband. He believes we owe him for the bad childhood he had. I don't see it that way. He drove us to distraction with his behaviour. He's the reason Bill had an asthma attack and died in my arms."

"What was the reason behind that? Did Dennis hurt your husband?"

"No, not physically. They got into a heated argument, tempers flaring and voices raised, and before long, the name-calling started. Dennis said some really unkind things to his father that he shouldn't have. I will never forgive him for that. I sit here most days, replaying that fateful day in my head and getting myself into a state all over again. But he's my son, and when he comes to visit, I always try to make exceptions for his rudeness. He's under a lot of pressure at work and has two teenage sons who are becoming a handful. Anyway, I'm sorry, you don't want to hear about my family issues. What is it you want to know?"

"About any families in particular who may have been relocated against their wills at the time the complex was built."

"Ah, yes. There was Mr Dyer. He lives over in Lugwardine now. Don't ask me what his address is; I couldn't tell you. He pops back now and again. Knocked on my door once or twice because he and Bill used to go to the pub together. Although, thinking about it, I've not seen him since Bill passed away."

"And he was angry about having to move home, was he?"

"He definitely was at the time. I should think he's calmed down these days. I suppose I'd feel just as aggrieved at having to leave my home. Let me think now. Yes, there was Mr Yates. He was taken to the hospital with a heart problem due to the stress. That actually happened during the move. His family had to rally around and get all his possessions out of the house. They made it with minutes to spare before the bulldozers tore up the place. That was a terrible situation to witness. The way some of the residents, those less capable, were treated. There were members of the council showing up periodically, knocking on people's doors, pestering folks, ensuring they would be out of their homes in time. Lots of animosity towards them from what I can remember. It wasn't their fault. It was that committee who gave the go-ahead for the complex to be built. They're the ones who were to blame. A lot of people at the time said they took backhanders to get it through the planning. It failed to get the permission needed a few times. The residents rejoiced every time it failed. Then all of a sudden, out of the blue, the permission was granted."

"How awful. Thank you for being so honest with us. You've given us the insight needed to delve deeper into what went on during the development stage of the complex."

"It was a nightmare around here for years. Off the top of my head, I think it took over two years to complete, much longer than anticipated, which infuriated the residents who were left. We had to endure early morning noise. The beep-beep-beep of the forklift trucks going back and forth, day in, day out. The only blessing was that they didn't work at the weekends. But then, at seven o'clock on Monday morning, it was back to it. The messy roads in the winter were disgusting. You see some sites these days, with the site being cleaned up by a street cleaner, but that wasn't the case back then. We had to replace our carpets every six months. That might be a slight exaggeration, but you know what it's like having two men in the house who refuse to take their shoes off at the front door. I was livid most weeks. I had a full-time job in a bank and still had to come home to muddy footprints on the carpet every night. In the end, I told Bill to take the carpets up in the hallway. If you were to pull them back now, you'd still see the evidence on the underlay of what we had to put up with."

"Oh dear. I'm sorry you had to contend with that kind of treatment."

Mrs Thatcher curled her lip and shook her head. "Seriously, you can't imagine what we went through."

"I think I can. Any building work can have a huge impact on the community. I bet it was a relief when it was finished."

"You could say that. Some of us struggled to get our lives back, though. The news kept filtering through that a couple of the men who were relocated had committed suicide."

"Oh no, how distressing for you all. Was that because they had to move their families?"

"That's right. It was never the same for them again. Being forced out of their homes like that, not being able to stand up for their family's rights. Bullied, that's what they were, bullied into moving. Setting up home in a different area, losing all that was familiar to them: neighbours, friends, the location. Some of them even lost their jobs. To some people, it was all they knew."

"I understand. It must have ripped their families apart. Can you give me any other names?"

"Let me think. You know how the memory plays up as you get older. Let me get into the zone." After a moment's thinking, she rose from her chair and walked across the room to a sideboard. She retrieved a notebook and returned to her seat. The old lady winced as she lowered herself into the chair.

"I could have got that for you," Sara suggested.

"Nonsense. Use it or lose it is my motto at my time of life. What do we have here? I've been meaning to update my address book for years. I cross out the people who have passed, and the names are getting fewer and fewer nowadays. Get your notebook ready."

Sara smiled at the kind woman. "I'm ready when you are."

"I've already mentioned Paul Dyer and Warren Yates. Let's see who else I can find here for you. Ah, yes, there's Ian Henshaw and his wife, Nell. I haven't got their phone numbers, only their addresses. They moved to fifteen Leyland Avenue in Eign Hill. I haven't got a forwarding address for the other two men, though. Sorry about that. Then there were Maurice and Cheryl Swanson. They moved to Lower Eggleton. Twenty-four Forest Road." She flicked through the rest of the book and shook her head. "All the others are dead now, unfortunately."

"You've been amazing. This will keep the investigation going for a while. I can't thank you enough for supplying us with so much insight and information."

"It's nice to feel appreciated after all these years. I truly hope something comes of it. Me being nosey, I have to ask what your investigation is really about. You said it spanned back twenty years, but you didn't tell me the significance about that era. Care to share with me? I completely understand if you can't, or if you don't want to."

"It's fine. Brace yourself, it's not pleasant."

"Oh my. Okay, consider me braced."

Sara looked the woman in the eye and said, "We're investigating three murders that have happened in the city over the last week."

Mrs Thatcher's colour drained from her rosy cheeks. She covered her mouth with her hand and gasped. Lowering her hand, she said, "And you believe there's a connection to these people, my friends and neighbours, being displaced?"

Sara sighed and nodded. "Yes, it seems the most likely possibility."

"My, my, my. I can't believe it. Mind you, those people really suffered. They were harassed beyond words to leave their homes. It shouldn't be allowed. Councils shouldn't have the authority to rip your house from under you like that. The tenants had rights; sadly, they meant nothing in the end. Shame on all those concerned who were on that committee; they stripped the residents of more than their homes that day. They were bullied, not allowed to speak out about the injustice of it all, while the people of the committee took backhanders and lined their pockets from the developers. Beggars belief, but it's true."

Sara suddenly felt awkward, knowing that Carla's father was one of those people. She stood and said, "Stay there, we'll show ourselves out. Thank you for all the valuable information you've supplied us with today."

Mrs Thatcher insisted on showing them to the door so that she could apply the chain for safety reasons. "I hope you solve the investigation before anyone else loses their life."

"So do we. Take care of yourself."

"I will. Good luck." She closed the door behind them.

Sara walked several paces, then stopped and touched Carla on the arm. "Are you all right? You went a bit quiet back there."

Carla's lips twisted as she bit them. Finally, she admitted, "No, I feel like shit. I'm desperate to get the truth out of my father, and if he were in better health, I'd rush over there and force it out of him. What the fuck, Sara? What the actual fuck is going on here?"

Sara stretched her arms out, and Carla walked into them.

"I'm sorry you're having to deal with this. I don't have all the answers yet. None of us do. I think we've uncovered enough information now to do the extra digging we need to get to the bottom of this. Even if it takes us working through the night, I'm determined to get to the truth."

"But we've tried. I don't know what else we can do. There's obviously been a major cover-up going on about this for years."

Sara winked at her. "Where there's a will. Come on, let's tell the others to call it a day and we'll head back to the station. Are you sure you're okay? Do we need to stop off for a stiff drink somewhere?"

"Christ, the way I'm feeling, if we did that, I wouldn't stop drinking until I was flat on my back, making a damn fool of myself."

Sara smiled. "The thing you need to remember is not to take this to heart. None of this is your fault."

"Yeah, right, but it is something to do with my father. What if he took backhanders and everything he and Mum have achieved over the years has been off the back of those funds?"

"You don't know that. Let's put that type of speculation aside for now, at least until your father is better."

"And if he doesn't survive? This will play on my mind forever."

"It needn't. Hey, you have enough on your plate with your wedding coming up. Plus, you're going to have to forget about the investigation when you visit your father, otherwise he's going to sense there is something wrong, and it could put his recovery back weeks, possibly months."

"Why do you always talk a lot of sense?"

Sara fluttered her eyelashes. "Because I'm a decent person and also your boss."

"Yeah, I knew that last part would feature somewhere in your response. Can we stop off at our secret café, without the others?"

"You've got it. Much better for us to have a flat white and a cream cake than alcohol during the day. I'm buying."

"No, this is on me. No arguments."

.   .   .

WHEN THEY ARRIVED at the café, Sara let her partner take care of the bill, and she sat at the table, observing her while she queued up.

"There you go. Are you sure you didn't want a cake to share?"

"I'm not in the mood, are you?"

"No, it would probably get stuck in my throat. I'm sorry to be on such a downer. For some reason, I feel responsible."

Sara took a sip of her coffee and then placed a hand over her partner's. "Stop it. None of this is your fault, or your father's."

Carla's eyes watered. "We don't know that. If my father was on this committee and the killings are related to it, then he's definitely involved, whether he realises it or not. I feel so frustrated that I can't tackle him about it, or Mum for that matter."

Sara wagged her finger. "You mustn't say anything to your mother. She has enough on her plate, worrying about your father."

"I know. I'm telling you, if he weren't in hospital, I'd be round there like a shot, demanding to know what his involvement was in all of this."

"Giving him the benefit of the doubt, maybe he doesn't know. Perhaps he was on the fringe of things, not one of the main players in the deal. Maybe he got talked into making the decision."

"You're being kind. I'd rather you didn't make excuses for him."

"I'm not, far from it. I'm only doing what I would usually do if faced with the same situation involving someone else."

Carla twisted her cup in the saucer. "I'm lost for words, and I have no thoughts either way on the subject. There was always something there with my father that I could never put my finger on."

"Really? You're not just saying it?"

"No. I wouldn't say we've been close over the years. Of course I love him; however, it was always Mum I turned to for advice or if I had a problem that needed solving. From what I can remember, he was never around that much. He worked as a councillor during the day and was involved in all sorts of clubs and activities in the evening. There were some days when I didn't see him at all."

Sara frowned. "Didn't your mother mind?"

"No. I think that's why she spent a lot of time with me, to make up for his absence."

"I'm sorry you had to put up with that. Makes you wonder why some people have kids if they refuse to spend time with them."

"Exactly. Anyway, I don't want to make this all about me and hold a pity party. We need to figure out what to do next."

"When we get back to the station, I think our main priority should be trying to find the people on the list Mrs Thatcher gave us."

"I agree. It seems bizarre to believe that the three victims have lost their lives this week because of something that happened twenty years ago. I wonder if we could have a talk with any police officers who were around at the time."

Sara raised a finger. "You might have something there. I think I'll call one of the journalists I've got to know recently and ask him if he can shed any light on anything."

"I know that our determination will help us get to the bottom of this."

Sara chinked her cup against Carla's. "I'll drink to that. Let's sup up and get out of here."

BACK AT THE STATION, the team went the extra mile to find the people on the list and came up trumps by the end of the day. Sara had left them to it and got to work trying to locate anyone at the station who was around at the time. She'd even called on Jeff to help out. He came up with a couple of names of sergeants who were long retired. One man was suffering from dementia and was at the end of his life in a care home. The other sergeant had moved out of the area, and Jeff was doing his best to locate him. That left Sara free to speak to the journalist she had become closer to in the past few months. They had a love-hate relationship that she was hoping to improve, for mutual backscratching purposes in the future.

"Hi, Lee. It's DI Sara Ramsey. How are you?"

"Oh, really? I suppose the answer to that would be *suspicious*. Why would you be calling me out of the blue, Inspector?"

"No need for you to be suspicious. I'm hoping you can help a struggling officer out. Are you up for it?"

"Intriguing. Tell me more."

"Well, as you know, we're in the middle of an ongoing investigation..."

"Wait, this wouldn't have anything to do with the conference you called the other day?"

"Correct. While we received a few calls from the public, they haven't really led anywhere. However, something has come to our attention that we're struggling to get our heads around, and I wondered if you'd be willing to help us out."

"Me? Well, this is a first for you, Sara Ramsey."

She ground her teeth at his arrogance and the fact that she'd had to sink this low to ask for his help. She laughed to break through the atmosphere that had developed between them. "Will you help me?"

"It depends."

"On what?"

"On whether our relationship is going to change from this day forward."

Sara's brow wrinkled in confusion. She covered the mouthpiece of the phone and blew out a breath. "I'm open to that," she eventually said. She closed her eyes and envisaged him grinning like a Cheshire cat and rubbing his hands together with glee.

*Right now, I'm willing to sell my soul to the Devil if it will help!*

"We should meet. Do you want me to come there, to the station?"

"No. I'd rather meet on neutral ground if you don't mind. How are you fixed now?"

"I can't just drop everything just because you summon me, Inspector."

"I wasn't asking you to. Are you busy?"

"I'm always busy."

"Ditto. What about after work, then? What time do you finish?"

"Around five-thirty. Do you have a favourite pub where we could meet?"

"Yes, the Sailor's Arms, on the edge of town. Do you know it?"

"I think so. I'll meet you there at five forty-five. How about that?"

"I'll look forward to it. I must dash; we've got a big story breaking in Worcester."

"If you can't make it, call me."

"I'll do that. TTFN."

Sara ended the call and shuddered at the thought of doing business with him. Yes, they'd had a few less aggressive meetings of late, but there had always been a 'gunning for the throat' attitude about him that she found off-putting, and now she was about to get into bed with the man. Figuratively speaking.


PLEASED WITH THE team's progress, Sara sent them on their way and glanced at her watch. It was five-thirty.

"Do you want me to come with you? I don't mind," Carla asked.

"No. I think he'll be more open if I meet him alone. You'll want to get to the hospital to see how your father is, anyway, won't you?"

Carla's chin dropped to her chest. "Not really. I know I have to go, out of obligation, but after what we've heard today, all I want to do is confront him."

"Rein it in, Carla. He's an ill man. Once he's released and on the road to recovery, then you can tackle him. I'm not saying we wouldn't find what he has to tell us useful for the investigation, but from what we've gathered so far, the pieces are beginning to slot together nicely without the need to bother him."

"Yeah, but it's a slow process. Talking to my father could speed things up considerably."

"Don't fret about it. Right, I've got to fly. Wish me luck."

"Good luck. Don't get shafted by the tosser. Don't let him hoodwink you into thinking he's got you wrapped around his little finger just because you need some information from him."

Sara smiled. "Thanks for the advice. I'll bear it in mind. Damn, I forgot to call Mark to warn him I'll be late home. I'll do it in the car. Give your parents my love, won't you?"

"I will. Thanks for being so understanding, Sara."

"You're my mate as well as my colleague. Now shoo!"

Carla left the incident room first. Sara checked everything was switched off and closed the door behind her. She walked through the reception area and out to the car. Once she was on the road, she rang Mark. His phone went straight to voicemail, which was unusual. *He must be in surgery.* She left him a message that she was meeting an important witness and that she would be home in an hour or so.

Lee was getting out of his vehicle when she drew into the car park. He smiled and waited for Sara to get out of her car to join him.

"Good evening, Lee. Thanks again for taking time out to meet me."

"I'm sure you'll make it worth my while. Drinks are on you, aren't they?"

She smiled. "Of course."

They entered the pub, and Sara pointed to a table in a secluded corner of the bar.

She gave him a twenty and said, "I'll have a glass of Sauvignon, thanks."

"What about snacks?"

"Not for me. Get what you want."

Sara sat on the bench seat, staring at the roaring fire in the inglenook, all sorts bombarding her mind. The main thought was that she was already regretting meeting him alone. She glanced over at the bar. He peered over his shoulder and smiled at her. She resisted the temptation to shudder and removed her phone from her pocket to check her personal emails until Lee arrived with their drinks.

"That's the trouble with coppers: you're like us, you never switch off."

Sara placed her phone on the table. "That's true."

He slid the drink across the table towards her and opened a packet of cheese and onion crisps. "Do you want one?"

"No, thanks. It'll put me off my dinner."

"Hubby at home, knocking that up for you now, is he?"

"No. He's in surgery."

"Surgery? Is he a doctor?" Lee asked. He downed a third of his beer in one gulp.

"He's a vet, a very successful one, too."

"I don't doubt it. Married to you. You always come across as someone who strives for perfection. Do you?"

Sara held his gaze. "I suppose so. Can we get down to business?"

"Cut out all the small talk, you mean? Where's the fun in that, Inspector? I thought our meeting tonight was a way for us to get to know each other more intimately, shall we say?"

"Sorry if I gave you that impression, Lee. This is an after-work meeting, nothing more."

"You disappoint me."

Her cheeks warmed up under his intense gaze.

He tipped his head back and laughed. "Sorry, I couldn't resist it. I'm messing with you."

Sara rolled her eyes and sighed. "I'm not here to be messed around. I reached out to you for help with a very important investigation, and here you are, treating it as an opportunity to wind me up." She picked up her handbag and stood.

He grabbed her wrist. "Please don't go. I'm sorry, I didn't mean to offend you."

She dropped down on the bench again. "You haven't."

"Okay. How can I help?"

"I can't go into specific details about the deaths. I know you're hoping for an exclusive on that front. Although this is to do with finding the killer of the three victims..."

"Wait! Three victims? So, there has been yet another murder. Is that what you're saying?"

Sara didn't react, although inside she kicked herself black and blue. "Yes, we discovered another body today. What I need your help with specifically is something that took place twenty years ago."

His eyes narrowed, and he took another gulp of his beer. "Like you, I wasn't living in Hereford back then."

"I thought I'd reach out to you in case you knew a journalist from around that time. Someone who you might trust."

He mulled over her suggestion for a few moments while he stuffed his face with yet more crisps. After a while, he nodded. "There might be. I haven't been in touch with him for a while. In fact, I'm not sure if he still lives in the area."

"Can you try and call him for me?"

"I haven't got his details with me. I can certainly try to reach him in the morning. Although, you're going to need to give me more to go on."

Sara sighed. "Okay, here's what we've got so far. But first, you have to promise me that the information I'm about to give you won't appear in the paper."

He shrugged. "You're asking a lot, but all right, I agree. I know most coppers don't like getting into bed with journalists, but at the end of the day, we're usually after the same thing: to keep Hereford safe."

"We are?" she asked doubtfully.

"Absolutely. We care about what happens in our community. All we want is to make the towns we live in a safer environment for the inhabitants. That's your main aim too, isn't it?"

Sara nodded. "Yes, I've never really thought about it that way before, not from your stance, I mean."

"See, we're generally misunderstood, especially by coppers. Maybe we can work together to change that in the future?"

"It's possible. Depends on how well we work together during this investigation. So, what I'm trying to find out is what went on twenty years ago when a housing estate was bulldozed."

His head bobbed up and down as she spoke. "The one out at Belmont, is that what we're talking about here?"

"Yes, that's the one."

"What have you uncovered so far?"

"It has to be off the record, Lee. I'm trusting you to do the right thing here."

"Okay, I'll cross my heart and hope to die if that will help you trust me."

Sara laughed, feeling more at ease as she sat opposite him. "That did the trick. Go on then, I'm waiting."

He amused her by doing the actions and saying the words in a toddler's voice. "Satisfied?" he asked.

"Very. Right, what we've discovered so far is that the three victims were part of a committee that was behind the demolition of the housing estate."

"Is that right? And now you're investigating who would have the motive to go after these people, is that it?"

"Sort of. What we're more interested in is the fact that during our research, the only article we could find in the archives wasn't very informative."

"As if a cover-up had happened?"

"It seems that way. Today, my team and I canvassed the estate opposite and spoke to some of the older residents who lived there twenty years ago. They intimated that there were a lot of backhanders going on at the time."

He raised his eyebrows. "Why am I not surprised to hear that? People working for the council and on some of these committees are the pits, at least that's my experience. Obviously, not everyone is the same, but you're bound to get the odd few who let the power they have at their fingertips go to their heads. So now it's come back to haunt them."

Sara sighed and nodded. "So it would seem. We need to know more about what went on at the time before we can flush out the killer. So far, he's not left any clues and has used false plates on the vehicles we have caught on CCTV footage we've viewed. Plus, he's given at least one fake name."

"So, you feel like your backs are against the wall, and that's why you've reached out to me for help?"

"As you said yourself, we're both after the same thing."

"Let me see what I can do for you in the morning. I'm not promising anything, though. I haven't been in touch with Dan for a number of years. His contact details might be obsolete by now."

"Please, all I'm asking is that you do what you can to help. There's a serial killer out there on a mission."

"What about the other members of the committee? Have you told them?"

Sara ran her finger around the edge of her glass. "Again, we're trying to locate them. One of them is my partner's father. She tried to talk to him about the situation... umm... I shouldn't really be telling you this."

"Go on. We've already established that you can trust me."

"He's in hospital after suffering a heart attack."

"Shit! That reeks of guilt, doesn't it?"

"It does. It has put my partner in a dilemma about how to proceed."

"I bet it has. Is her father bad?"

"Fortunately, it was a mild heart attack, but it's his involvement in this that she's struggling to handle."

"I totally get that. I think I'd feel the same. Is she close to her father?"

"Yes and no. The truth is slowly coming out. She's appalled that this situation has come to a head."

Lee tilted his head to ask, "Is he at risk? From the killer?"

"Who knows? We've taken the precaution of putting a guard on his door."

"I don't blame you." He downed the rest of his drink and scrunched up his empty crisp packet. "Leave it with me. I'll do some digging and get back to you by midday at the latest."

Sara smiled and emptied her glass. "Thanks, I really appreciate your help."

He winked at her. "You owe me, just remember that."

They left the table.

Sara laughed. "Are you likely to allow me to forget?"

"Er, no. You can trust me, Sara, I promise you."

"I'm glad to hear it. Thanks for meeting me, Lee. It was good getting to know you."

"Have you?"

"Well, maybe not. You know what I mean."

They walked back to their cars.

He held her door open for her while she got in. "We'll catch up tomorrow. Enjoy the rest of your evening. Umm... before you go, can I ask how your new DCI is working out? I bet that came as a shock, finding out his predecessor was bent."

She smiled and said, "It's still early days yet. He seems a fair chap. Enjoy your evening, too." She closed the door before he could ask any further awkward questions about Price and her downfall. However, during her drive home, she pushed that aside and suddenly felt more confident about her current case. Despite her reservations, the evening had turned out to be a success as far as she was concerned. It remained to be seen whether Lee would stick to his word, although she wasn't aware of any warning signs that had reared their heads during their meeting.

*Let's see what tomorrow brings.*

She rang Mark. He picked up, sounding harassed.

"Sorry, have I caught you at a bad time?"

"No. Sorry. I lost a dog during an operation this evening. I've just got off the phone with the owners."

"Oh no, how dreadful. I'm so sorry, Mark. Was the dog old?"

"Yes, he was twelve. He was going blind as well. They let him off at the park, and he got attacked by another dog. The injuries were too severe to save him. I told the owners that, but they wanted me to do what I could to save the poor dog."

"It's not your fault. Don't go blaming yourself if the injuries were life-threatening, darling."

"Easier said than done. I hate it when I lose a patient."

"I know. Are you going home now?"

"Yes. I have to clean up here first, though. How has your day been?"

"Interesting. I'm on my way home now. I'll see you later." She ended the call, feeling despondent for her husband. She was halfway home when her phone rang. "DI Sara Ramsey, how may I help?"

"It's me. Sorry to call so late. I've just finished the PM on Oliver Grant and thought I should ring you right away," Lorraine said.

"Oh, hi. I was wondering how you were getting on. What's up?"

"After I conducted a thorough examination of the victim, I found something interesting in his mouth."

"It has been a long day for both of us. Are you going to tell me what it was or keep me in suspense?"

"It turned out to be a note for you. No idea how it managed to remain in his mouth. Actually, I do. It was shoved to the back of his throat."

"Oh crap. Don't say that. That image will remain with me for the rest of the evening, now."

"Sorry. I didn't mean to upset you. Do you want to know what it says?"

"Of course."

*"Inspector Ramsey, do you dare uncover the truth? Look close to home."*

"What the fuck? So, the killer obviously knows we're on to him, probably because of the conference I held."

"That was my first thought, too. What about the last part of the message? Any ideas about that?"

"Possibly. It might be to do with Carla's father."

"Care to enlighten me, or are you going to turn the tables on me and keep me guessing?"

"Sorry, I was distracted. I'm getting close to home, just need to take a right turn across the oncoming traffic." She put her foot down and made the manoeuvre swiftly, only for the driver coming towards her to beep his horn.

"Pissing the other drivers off in the process, I see. Naughty you."

"Impatient bugger. I had plenty of time to turn, without him having to brake."

"Forget about your near miss. Any news on Carla's father and his part in the investigation? You hinted before that he might be involved."

Sara sighed and went over the details for the second time that evening.

"Shit! That's bad news. How is he?"

"I think he's doing all right. The doctor is monitoring the situation. He might need to have a stent put in or go through a heart bypass. It's unclear how they're going to proceed, yet."

"And how is Carla holding up?"

"She's frustrated as hell."

"I bet she is. I take it she's dying to grill him about his involvement."

"You'd be right about that. These things are sent to try us at the best of times."

"Ain't that the truth? Will you send her my best wishes and tell her to keep her chin up?"

"I'll do it in the morning. Are you calling it a day now?"

"Yep. I'll pick up a Chinese on the way home and flop onto the sofa for the rest of the evening. How come you're not home yet?"

"I had to meet with someone after work."

"Is that it? Aren't you going to tell me who you met?"

"You're a nosey bitch. If you must know, I met a journalist."

"What the fuck? Are you crazy? Well, he or she obviously didn't eat you alive, so that's a blessing. Was this to do with the investigation?"

Again, Sara divulged what had taken place during her meeting and winced as she waited for Lorraine to fly off the handle.

"I repeat, are you frigging crazy?"

"No. We have come to an understanding. I trust him."

"Bloody hell. You've lost the plot since I saw you this morning. You must have done."

"Thanks for flinging that insult my way. I think the world of you, too."

"I'm sorry. No offence, but since when did you have to rely on what a journalist can do for you to solve an investigation?"

"Since now. Something isn't right, and we need to get to the bottom of it before we can proceed. In our line of business, anything and everything goes, within reason, right?"

Lorraine puffed out a lengthy breath. "I never thought I'd see the day when the infamous DI Sara Ramsey would resort to asking a bloody journalist for help. I hope you know what you're doing and that it doesn't backfire on you."

"Thanks, I've got my fingers crossed it doesn't, as well. Enjoy your takeaway and the rest of your evening."

"You too. Speak soon."

"I'd think something was wrong if we didn't."

Having the conversation with Lorraine had planted a seed of doubt in her mind about whether she was indeed doing the right thing by working with Lee.

# 10

---

"How's your father doing?" Sara asked Carla the second she stepped out of her vehicle the following morning.

Carla spotted her pull into the car park and waited for her outside the main entrance to the station. She sighed. "He seemed a bit better last night, but the doctor warned us that he could go the other way if he didn't have an operation soon."

Sara stopped walking, shocked to hear the news. "I thought they were running tests on him?"

"They were. The doctor told my parents yesterday that Dad needs a stent."

"Well, that's not the end of the world, is it? I've heard it's not as invasive as a heart bypass, so that's a bonus, isn't it?"

Carla rubbed her hand around her chin. "Maybe. I don't know. Any surgical procedure gives me the jitters. What if he dies on the table?"

"Anyone can say that. All you need to do is remain positive, if only for your mother's sake. She's going to be relying on you to be there for her."

"I know." Carla blew out a breath and walked through the main entrance into the reception area. "Ignore me. I barely know what to think for the best at the moment."

"Hey, no one could blame you for thinking that way. You know where I am if you need to chat."

Carla gave her a half-smile. "I know. I appreciate it, Sara. How did your meeting shape up last night?"

"It was much better than expected. Lee is going to do some digging and get back to me later today."

"And he was confident about finding something useful?"

"I'd say more hopeful than confident. He knows a journalist who was around back in the day, although he's not quite sure where he lives now."

"Let's hope he can come up with the goods, because we haven't got much to go on as it is."

"Ain't that the truth? I want us to go over any loose ends we have, first thing. I'm sensing each time a murder comes our way, the investigation stalls."

"Hardly surprising, is it? We're getting snowed under, and I can't see a way out of our predicament."

They entered the security door and ascended the stairs to the incident room.

"We'll focus on the information we gathered yesterday and see what comes of it."

"Ah, DI Ramsey. Just the person I was looking for. Have you got time for a chat in my office?"

Sara rolled her eyes as soon as she heard the voice of DCI Blake behind her. Smile fixed in place, she turned to face him. "Of course, sir. Now?"

"That's what I said."

He walked back to his office and peered over his shoulder to make sure she was following.

"I shouldn't be long," she mumbled to Carla and jogged along the corridor to catch up with him.

Mary, the DCI's secretary, smiled and welcomed her. "Hello, Inspector. How are you?"

"Fine," she replied hesitantly. As soon as Blake entered his office, she whispered, "Any idea why I've been summoned?"

Mary shook her head. "Sorry. I haven't."

"DI Ramsey, I haven't got all day," he bellowed.

Sara shot into his office and closed the door behind her.

"Take a seat. There's no need for you to look so terrified."

"I'm not. Thanks, sir. How are you settling in?"

"I'm just about there. I was eager to find out how you're getting on with your investigation. I've heard on the grapevine that you're now dealing with three murders. Is that true?"

Sara sat opposite him and linked her hands together in her lap. "Unfortunately, yes. We're linking all three murders; therefore, you know as well as I do what that signifies."

"Hereford has yet another serial killer on the loose. Not something I envisaged having to deal with during my first week in the area. How is the investigation going?"

"The only thing I can tell you is that it's progressing slowly. The team is doing their best but, as I'm sure you can appreciate, having to attend another murder scene puts us behind considerably. We're stretched to the limits." *We're not, but it doesn't hurt to say it.*

"Is there anything I can do to help? Would you reach out to me if you were struggling? Or are you the type to keep your head down in the hope that I don't notice you?"

Sara frowned and sat upright. "Not at all, sir. I'm doing my very best. We all are. If you have any qualms about the speed at which the investigation is progressing, then all I can do is apologise. My team and I have always solved cases quickly, unlike some other teams in the area."

"It wasn't a criticism. I'm genuinely offering you a hand if you need it. Please, don't be afraid to ask."

"I won't, sir." She went on to fill him in on what they were up against.

"Do you have any suspects in mind at all?"

"Not really, not yet. We're going to knuckle down today and go through the list of displaced residents that one of the ladies on a nearby estate told us about yesterday. Hopefully, that will lead us somewhere."

"Do you believe Carla's father is in danger?"

"The truthful answer to that is that I'm not sure. I have an officer on guard outside his room, which, for now, is giving us all peace of mind."

"That's good. I was about to suggest the same. What about the other members of the committee? Have you managed to find them yet?"

"Again, it's something we're looking into at present."

"All right. Well, you seem to have it covered for now. Don't forget to give me a shout if you need any advice or assistance." He winked at her. "Between you and me, I quite enjoy getting my hands dirty now and again."

Sara smiled and left her seat. "I'll bear it in mind, sir. I'd better get on with my day. I hold a morning meeting with my team every day."

"In that case, I apologise for holding you up, Inspector. I hope you have a productive day."

"Thank you, sir." Sara left the office and closed the door behind her. She stood against it and shut her eyes.

"Is everything all right, Sara?" Mary asked.

"Yes, I think so. I was so apprehensive that I worked myself up into a state before I went in there. This is my relieved status."

They both laughed.

"From what I've seen of him so far, I don't think he's going to be the type of boss who will come down heavily on you if you make a mistake."

"We'll have to see about that. Hey, what are you saying? That I've screwed up a lot under Price's leadership?"

"Oh, heavens. I wouldn't dare to insinuate such a thing. I'm so sorry for opening my big mouth."

Sara took a few steps towards her. "I'm joking. Fingers crossed he works out for all of us. You more than anyone."

"Let's hope so."

She returned to the incident room with a determination that she was lacking when she'd arrived at the station half an hour before.

"Right, where are we?" she asked the second she set foot in the incident room.

"We've located a couple of the names Mrs Thatcher gave us yesterday," Carla said. "Have you had a coffee?"

"Not yet, and yes, I'd love one, thanks."

Carla made the drink and handed it to her. "How did it go with the chief?" she whispered.

"Surprisingly well. I'm not getting the impression that he's going to be a pest during an investigation."

"That remains to be seen. Do you want to venture out and have a chat with some of these people?"

"You read my mind. I'll give my post and emails a cursory look through while I drink my coffee, and then we'll get on the road. Will you do the necessary and carry out a brief background check on their social media networks?"

"Blimey, you're not expecting much, are you?"

Sara grinned and walked into her office. "Actually, I am," she shouted over her shoulder and closed the door behind her. No sooner had she taken a seat than her office phone rang. "DI Sara Ramsey. How may I help?"

"It's Jeff, ma'am. I wanted to let you know that my men responded to a nine-nine-nine call this morning. A stabbing which might have been a lot worse had the attacker not been disturbed by the victim's wife."

"That's unfortunate, Jeff. Your team is going to have to deal with it. We're totally snowed under already."

"I appreciate that. Sorry, I wouldn't involve you unnecessarily, ma'am. You should know that by now."

"Go on." She blew on her coffee and took a sip.

"The victim is Eddie Lawton. I recognised the name and did the necessary research on him. He used to be a councillor."

"Shit! Okay, you'd better give me his address?"

The desk sergeant shared the information and added, "He's been taken to the A and E Department."

"Thanks. Carla and I will pop over and have a word with him. You did the right thing informing me, Jeff. Sorry to have doubted you."

"Thanks, ma'am."

Sara took another sip of her steaming-hot drink, groaned at having to leave it and raced out of the room. "Carla, grab any addresses we need to visit while we're out. First, we're going to visit a victim who has been stabbed. He's been rushed to the hospital. Before you ask, he's an ex-councillor."

"Ouch! So, a possible victim to add to the list."

"Exactly. His address is eighteen St Peter's Drive. Craig, can you go over any possible footage or cameras in the area while we're out?"

"Consider it done, boss."

They ran down the stairs and out to Sara's car.

"My paperwork is piling up," she complained, then dropped behind the steering wheel.

"The new chief will have to accept it if victims keep coming our way. How come the killer left this guy alive?"

"He was disturbed during the attack. That's as much as I know about what happened."


THE A and E Department was surprisingly quiet when they arrived. Sara showed her ID to the receptionist, who had already recognised her.

"Ah, yes. Mr Lawton is in triage right now. His wife is the lady in the green coat, sitting at the end."

"Brilliant. Thanks very much. We'll have a chat with her. Any news on how her husband is?"

The receptionist screwed up her nose. "It's too soon to tell yet."

"Not to worry."

Sara and Carla walked across the area, and Sara introduced herself to the woman who was clearly shaken up.

"Hello, Mrs Lawton. I'm DI Sara Ramsey, and this is my partner,

DS Carla Jameson. Sorry this happened to your husband. Is there any news on him, yet?" she asked, despite already knowing the answer.

"No, not yet. We got here ten minutes ago, so I suppose it's too soon for them to have any news for me." Tears dripped onto her cheeks, and she wiped them away with a tissue. "Please forgive me. I feel foolish for getting so upset. But Eddie means the world to me. We've been together since our schooldays."

"It's fine, have a good cry if you need to. Don't hold back on our account. Can you tell us how your husband was attacked?"

"He told me he was going out to water the plants in the greenhouse. It's that time of year when the seedlings are doing well and will need potting on soon. Anyway, I leave him to it for ten minutes or so, then usually take him a cup of tea. The greenhouse is at the bottom of our garden. I turned the corner and looked up to see a man with his hand raised, attacking my husband. I didn't know what to do for the best, so I screamed. The man was so shocked he dropped the weapon and ran off."

"Do you still have the weapon?"

"I thought you might ask that. Yes, I picked it up with my apron and hid it in the greenhouse. Did I do the right thing? It all happened so quickly. It's hard to know what's right or wrong when a situation like this crops up."

Sara smiled. "Yes, you did the right thing. Did you notice if the man was wearing gloves at all?"

"Ah, I'm not sure. I suppose I should have taken notice. How silly of me. But then, after he'd run off, my priority was to tend to my husband. Fortunately, Eddie carries his phone with him wherever he goes, that's why I was able to call for an ambulance right away. Then I tended to my husband's wound. The attacker stabbed him in the chest. The paramedics praised my quick thinking when they arrived. They told me that Eddie probably wouldn't have survived if I hadn't pressed firmly on his wound. Years ago, when I was at work, members of the St John Ambulance came to the supermarket and ran a weekly course for us. If I hadn't taken part in that training... well, I'm sure you can imagine how it would have ended."

"That's excellent. Glad you saved the day and your husband's life."

She shook her head. "Don't be too quick to praise me. We don't know how Eddie is yet or whether he's going to survive."

Sara gathered the woman's hand in her own. "No, that's true. But you were there, and as the paramedic told you, your ability to know what to do probably ended up saving Eddie's life."

"We'll see. It was horrendous being put in that situation. At first, I was so confused and I had no idea what to do for the best. I had to take a few deep breaths to calm myself down."

"I'm sure. You did amazingly well. I'm glad your training came in handy."

"The paramedic said Eddie wouldn't be here today if I hadn't jumped in."

"There you go, then. Not all heroes or heroines wear capes."

Mrs Lawton smiled. "I needed to hear that. Thank you for coming so quickly. Is there a reason a detective has shown up instead of a uniformed officer to take down my statement?"

"Actually, there is. We were told your husband used to be a councillor in the area, is that true?"

"Yes. He gave up a couple of years ago. Well, when I say gave up, what I should have said was that he took retirement."

"I see. Well, we've been investigating several murders that have happened this week. The victims were all part of a committee that we believe your husband was on, as well."

"What? And someone has a grievance against the members, is that it? Who else has died? Do I know them?"

"Richard Manning, Alan Fletcher and Oliver Grant. Do the names ring a bell with you?"

"Vaguely, although I don't believe it's because they were Eddie's colleagues on the council."

"No, but all the men were on this committee that we believe has links to the council."

"Okay, then that would make sense. Oh dear. And they're all dead, you say? And the killer, you believe he was the one who attacked my husband?"

"It's possible."

She sniffled and wiped her nose on a clean tissue. "But my husband is a good man. At least, I've always believed him to be. Why would this person set out to try to kill him?"

"We've yet to discover the motive for the crimes he's committed. We're doing our best to establish the truth behind the murders. Is it possible for you to give us a description of this man?"

"I only caught a brief glance of him before he vaulted over our fence. I'd say he was in his late teens or early twenties, although saying that, who can tell these days?"

"That's great. It's a start, and more than we've managed to find out about him so far. Any idea of his weight and height? I know it's probably asking a lot of you."

"He was lean. I'd say more on the thin side. He reminded me of people who take drugs. They never seem healthy to me. Maybe I'm talking nonsense, but it's the best I can do off the top of my head. As for his height, it was difficult to tell. Our fence is six feet. I suppose he was several inches taller than that but, then again, I couldn't tell you that for definite. He must be pretty fit to have got over it on the first attempt. He didn't look back, so I couldn't tell you what his features were like, not really. He didn't have any facial hair, if that helps."

Sara nodded. "It does. You're doing incredibly well."

A doctor came towards them. Sara paused her questions to listen to what he had to tell Mrs Lawton.

"Hello. I'm Doctor Nicholl. I thought I'd come and give you an update about your husband. He's going down to the operating theatre soon. The knife missed his heart, but we need to take a look inside in case any other organs were touched during the attack. He seems pretty upbeat in there. He's been asking for you, Mrs Lawton. We'll move him to a cubicle soon, once we've cleaned him up a little, so you'll be able to see him. If you hadn't been on the scene, I can tell you this: he probably wouldn't have survived."

"I just did what any other human being would have done faced with the same situation."

The doctor shook his head. "I don't believe that's true in the slightest. I'll get back to it. A nurse or porter will come and fetch you soon." He walked away.

Mrs Lawton covered her face with her hands and sobbed, letting out all the pent-up emotions that had been bubbling under the surface since she arrived.

"Let it out. It must be such a relief to hear he's going to be okay," Sara said. She placed an arm around the woman's shoulders.

"I feel such an idiot breaking down like this. I'm not the crying type. Eddie would tell you as much. But you're right, I feel nothing but relief."

A few seconds later, a hospital bed was pushed into the corridor and into a cubicle.

"It's him. That's my husband. Please excuse me, won't you?"

"Of course. We'll give you a couple of minutes."

She crept along the corridor, pulled back the curtain to the cubicle and stepped inside.

"What are we going to do now?" Carla asked.

"We'll give them some time then see if Eddie is up to speaking with us."

Carla groaned. "I doubt it. He's waiting for surgery, Sara. It wouldn't be right to push him."

"I have no intention of putting pressure on him."

Carla folded her arms and stretched out her legs, crossing them at the ankles. "I'd be livid if you intruded on my privacy if I were that poorly."

"All right, you've made your point. Do I have to remind you that we have a serial killer on the loose out there?"

Carla sat upright and stared at her. "Of course you don't."

"Why are you being so anal about this, then? Does it have anything to do with your father being in hospital?"

Carla sighed. "Sorry. Maybe. It's not intentional, I promise. I suppose being here and not being able to visit him is getting to me."

"We can remedy that. Go. I can hang around here for half an hour or so with the Lawtons."

Carla leaned over and kissed her on the cheek. "You're the best. I won't be long."

"You'd better not be. Give them my love."

"I will."

She watched Carla tear down the corridor towards the lift. She waved at Sara before the doors closed. Sara gave her a thumbs-up, picked up a magazine from the table beside her and flicked through it until Mrs Lawton appeared. She gestured for Sara to join them. Sara shot out of her chair. She didn't need to be asked twice.

"Eddie wants to speak to you," Mrs Lawton whispered before they entered the cubicle.

"If you're sure. I won't put him under too much pressure."

"He wants to see you. Go ahead and ask your questions. Let's see how it goes for now, shall we?"

"Hello, Mr Lawton. I'm so sorry this happened to you but extremely glad you've survived the attack."

He turned his head slowly on the pillow and smiled weakly. "So am I, believe me."

"It would be helpful if you answered a few questions for me, if you're up to it?"

"What do you want to know besides what my wife has already told you, Inspector?"

"Did the attacker say anything either before or during the attack?"

"He called me every name under the sun and some I didn't know."

"Did you recognise him?"

"Not at all. That's why I was so shocked, not only to see him standing in our garden but also because he was venting his anger on me. Wait, he did mention something that puzzled me."

Sara's interest piqued, and she withdrew her notebook from her pocket. "What was that?"

"He said he was doing it as justice for the residents. Do you know what he meant by that? I'm presuming it had something to do with my councillor days."

Sara explained what had taken place during the week and how far they had got with their investigation. "We believe this has to do with what went on twenty years ago."

He shook his head and sighed. "I had a feeling this would come back and haunt us one day."

"Oh, can you tell me more?"

"A couple of other committee members and I were bullied into changing not only our opinions on that decision but also our votes. It was all about the money. Those with the loudest voices on that committee were the ones who had more to gain than the rest of us."

"Are you suggesting people like Oliver Grant?"

"Yes, him and some of the others. I tried to fight the development, I truly did. I couldn't stand the thought of those residents being kicked out of their homes. The stress some of us were under was incredible. At the time, I had a visit from some very unsavoury men who helped persuade me to vote in favour of the scheme."

"What? Why didn't you tell me this, Eddie?" his wife demanded. She clutched his hand between hers.

"I couldn't. I should have been man enough to stand up to them. I wasn't. I not only let down the residents who were displaced, but also you, my love."

Mrs Lawton smoothed back his damp hair. "Nonsense. You could never let me down."

They shared a loving smile, which Sara found touching, but she was also impatient and eager to get on with the investigation.

"We've tried to uncover what went on but can't find anything substantial in the archives. All we have are a few statements from the residents living opposite the complex now. If you can fill in the missing blanks, that would really help us solve this case."

Eddie shared a worried glance with his wife. "I wish I could remember all the details, but I've lived a full life since then. I'm sorry."

"Eddie, are you telling the inspector the truth?"

"Of course I am." He tried to raise his head; however, exhaustion took over, and his eyes flickered shut. "So tired," he whispered before he passed out.

Frantic, Sara raced into the corridor and called out for assistance. "Help me, please. It's Mr Lawton."

Doctor Nicholl, accompanied by two nurses, came hurtling out of triage and pushed past Sara. "Please leave, Mrs Lawton."

"What's wrong with him? No, I want to wait here."

"Inspector, can you care for Mrs Lawton while we take her husband back into triage?"

Sara drew back the curtain and tugged on Mrs Lawton's arm. "Please, let them do their job. Come with me."

The poor woman was in shock. Her gaze drifted between all of them. Sara successfully got her to leave and encouraged her to take a seat in the corridor. They watched as her husband was wheeled back into triage.

Carla arrived back about five minutes later. She frowned and mouthed to Sara, "What's wrong?"

"Excuse me a moment, Mrs Lawton. Would you like a drink?"

"A cup of tea would be nice. Please, please can you use your influence to find out what's going on?"

"I'll try. Carla, can you get the drinks?"

Carla joined her, and they walked back to the reception area. En route, Sara brought her partner up to speed with what was going on.

"Crap. Is he going to be all right?" Carla asked.

"I wouldn't like to say. One minute he was chatting away to us, and the next he complained he was tired and passed out. Any news on your father?"

"No. He's pretty much the same. They're intending to do the operation in the morning."

"That's good news. How's your mother?"

"Fretting, in case he doesn't pull through it. I've told her he's in safe hands, but I don't think she believes me."

She rubbed Carla's arm. "I'm sure things will work out for the best. Let me check how Mr Lawton is. You grab us all a drink."

They separated at the reception desk.

"Sorry to be a nuisance, but Mr Lawton was taken back into triage a little while back. His wife is really concerned about him. I don't suppose you can tell me what's going on, can you?"

"Let me see what I can find out." The receptionist made a private phone call from another desk and returned to give Sara the news. "I'm sorry. The doctor is still assessing Mr Lawton. He told me to ask you to be patient and said that he'll be with you soon."

Sara sighed and smiled. "I thought that might be the case. I'll let his wife know."

"I hope Mr Lawton improves soon. Have faith. We have some of the best A and E doctors in the area."

"That's reassuring. Thanks."

Carla joined her with a small tray and three plastic cups. "Any news?"

"Nothing as yet. They've asked us to be patient."

"I hate it when they say that. That's all Mum ever hears," Carla replied quietly as they got closer to Mrs Lawton.

"Did you find out anything, Inspector?" Mrs Lawton rose from her seat and asked.

"I didn't. The doctor passed on a message that he's still assessing your husband and will report back to us as soon as he can."

Carla encouraged Mrs Lawton to take her seat again and handed her drink to her. "This will help."

"Thank you, dear. I hope they don't keep us waiting too long."

Sara's phone rang. She checked the caller ID. "Sorry, I have to take this. It's important."

Mrs Lawton waved her apology away.

Sara answered the call on the third ring. "DI Sara Ram..."

"Sara, it's me, Lee. Sorry, I'm going to have to keep this brief. As promised, I've done some digging. I found the file. It was archived at our end, and the file had been corrupted. I have a friend who has been able to gain access to it. I'm going to email it to you now."

"Damn. I'm out of the office. The killer struck again."

"Shit! Who was the victim this time?"

"Eddie Lawton. He was a councillor at the time. The killer screwed up; the victim survived. I'm at the hospital with him now. The doctor is assessing the damage after the killer stabbed him."

"He's a determined bastard. Yes, Edward Lawton's name was on the list."

"The signal can be dodgy around here at the best of times. I'll check if I can access my emails and go through the file. What about the journalist you mentioned? Any luck tracing him?"

"Yep. He now lives in Dorset. I rang him. At first, he was reluctant to talk to me, but as soon as I told him it was a matter of life and death for those who were on the committee, he sat up and listened to me. He said that he'd recently received a call from the son of a man who committed suicide shortly after he was forced to move his family from the estate."

"Wow, okay. Did he give you a name?"

"That's the thing. He's got early-onset dementia and couldn't remember."

"Bugger. All right, thanks for the call. I'll get my team on it ASAP."

"I knew you'd appreciate the information. Let me know how you get on."

"I will. Thanks, Lee." She pressed the End button and immediately rang the station. "Jill. It's me. Can you hear me? I'm going to need to speak quietly because of my surroundings."

"Yes, boss. Is everything all right?"

"It is. We're still at the hospital, awaiting news about the victim. Listen, I've received some valuable information from one of my sources. I need you to do some further digging for me."

"Sure. What do you need?"

"From the list Mrs Thatcher gave me of the families that were forcibly relocated, I need you to find a man who committed suicide and left a wife and son behind."

"Hang on, I might have that information for you already." The sound of ruffling papers filled the line. "Yes, here it is. Ian Henshaw, who was married to Nell and had a son called Alex. Mrs Thatcher actually gave us the wife's address, not sure where the son lives."

"Great job. Find out what you can about Alex and get back to me, please. As soon as we're able to leave here, we'll pay him and his mother a visit. Will you text me the address you have for them? I ripped it out of my notebook to give it to you."

"Absolutely. Fingers crossed your informant is correct."

"I hope so, too. Can you also have a chat with the desk sergeant? Ask Jeff to send another member of his team to the hospital to guard Lawton's room. He's supposed to go down for surgery shortly. As soon as that happens, we'll get on the road."

"I'll arrange that for you, boss. Let's hope we catch this bastard soon."

"I can sense we're getting closer. Speak later." Sara gestured for Carla to join her and revealed what she'd been told.

"That's great. We should get over there now. There's nothing more we can do here."

"I know you're right, but I'd hate to leave Mrs Lawton, especially when she's in a state."

"She won't mind, not if the prospect of arresting the killer is high."

Sara nodded. "Okay, you've persuaded me." Her phone tinkled, signalling that a message had arrived. She checked out the address. "It's only up the road, in Eign Hill. It wouldn't take us long to get there. If we draw a blank, we can nip back here."

"Sounds like a good plan to me. She won't mind; we should do it."

"I'll let her know we've had a possible sighting of the suspect. That should do." They wandered back to where Mrs Lawton was sitting, nursing her drink in her hand.

"Hello again. Was it about the investigation?" Mrs Lawton asked.

Sara spotted the hope materialise in her tearful eyes. "It was. We've had a sighting of the suspect; we need to check it out. I hate to leave you but..."

"Go. I'd rather you were out there, hunting down the bastard who did this, rather than sitting here with me. I'll be fine. Please don't worry about me."

"If you're sure. We'll be back to see you soon, I promise."

"There's no need. I would much rather you spent your time out there, searching for this despicable character."

Sara squeezed her shoulder. "We'll be thinking of you both."

Then she and Carla raced out of the hospital, paid the parking fee and jumped into the car.

Sara's heart pounded the closer they got to Eign Hill. "I don't know Leyland Avenue, do you?"

"I think I do. If you take a right and the next left, that should bring us to it."

Sara let out a relieved sigh when Carla's directions proved to be accurate. "Number fifteen, where are you?"

Carla pointed ahead. "There's a white van. I'm guessing that's the house. Umm... don't rip my head off, but do you think we should call for backup?"

"I'll put the call in, but I'd rather not hang around waiting for them to arrive."

Carla tutted and shook her head. "Sorry, I have to say this. I think you're wrong. We haven't even got any Tasers with us. How the heck are we going to bring down an armed serial killer?"

"Smartarse, okay. Let's sit here and observe from a distance for now. I'll ask Barry and Craig to join us and get them to bring their weapons with them. How's that?"

Carla grinned. "I'd feel much happier."

Sara rang the station again. The ever-enthusiastic Craig leapt at the chance to be in on the action. "Sign out a couple of Tasers. We'll see you shortly. Join us in the car when you get here."

"Yes, boss. We'll be ten minutes max."

"See you soon."

They continued to keep a close eye on the mid-terraced house until their colleagues arrived. Craig and Barry hopped into the back, and Sara revealed the plan she had conceived. "We should split up. Barry and Carla, you go round the back of the property, just in case he tries to make a run for it. Craig and I will take the front. That way, each couple will be armed. Don't be afraid to use your Taser on him if things escalate. Got that?"

Both men nodded.

"Right, let's go. Carla, why don't you and Barry head off first? Make out you're having a conversation as you walk past. Ring me when you're in position. Let me know what you've seen as you pass the house."

"Will do. Good luck," Carla said.

With her heart in her mouth, Sara watched as Carla and Barry walked arm in arm past number fifteen and disappeared out of sight at the end of the terrace. Her mobile rang. "Hi. What did you see?" She put the speaker on so they could both hear Carla's response.

"The curtains in the lounge were still drawn, so not much. We're in the alley at the rear. The curtains in the back bedroom are also closed."

"Great. So, if we knock now, we're probably going to wake them up. Stay alert, we're going in."

"Be careful," Carla warned unnecessarily.

"You too. Between us, we've got this." She ended the call and put her mobile in her jacket pocket. "Are you ready?"

"It's now or never, right?" Craig replied. "Wait... someone is leaving the house. It's him."

Sara withdrew her phone and rang Carla. "Change of plan. The suspect has just left the house. Get back to the car."

She drummed her fingers on the steering wheel as she watched Alex jump into his van and pull away. Carla and Barry rounded the corner and jogged back to them.

"We'll split up," Sara said. "Follow him. Play leapfrog with the vehicles in case he spots either of us. Go."

Craig shot out of the back, and Carla slipped into the passenger seat. Sara started the engine and put her foot down. The van took a right at the end of the road.

Sara followed it, with two other cars in between. "Looks like he's heading into town."

"Do we know where he works? Is he self-employed?"

"Get on to Jill and ask if she's found out anything about him yet."

Carla made the call and put the phone on speaker again. "He's a self-employed electrician. He's been in business for only six months. Before that, he worked in Worcester for another electrical firm."

"Okay, that makes sense and explains why he was at Grant's house, carrying out the work there. He's on the move. We'll keep you informed."

"Good luck," Jill shouted before Carla hit the End button.

"I wonder if he's on his way to collect supplies," Sara said.

"Either that or he's on his way to stalk and kill another victim," Carla replied with a grunt.

They continued to follow the van through the city. Sara kept up with him through the maze of traffic lights around the outskirts of town. He drew up outside an electrical supplier on one of the industrial estates.

"Do we wait or hit him now?" Carla asked.

"Let's hang fire for a while. If there are bystanders around, that could lead to further deaths or injuries."

Henshaw was inside the premises for around ten minutes. He left the building and looked directly at their vehicle. Then he ran to his van and roared away, scattering the gravel on the driveway in his wake.

"Bugger! He knows we're on to him." Sara slammed the car into gear and gave chase with Craig close on her tail.

Luckily, Henshaw chose to drive out into the country rather than risk getting caught up in the traffic around the city. He put his foot down and even went through a red light close to Morrisons.

"Flick on the siren."

The blues and twos helped to pave their way through the traffic. Henshaw showed no signs of slowing down. He drove through a small estate at speed, almost knocking over a mother pushing a pram.

"We've got to stop him before he kills someone."

"Want me to call for extra backup and get a stinger set up?" Carla asked.

"You can make the sergeant aware of the situation. Not sure about the stinger, not if he's going to lead us a merry dance driving through estates like this."

Carla made the call. Jeff advised them he would send two patrol cars to their location.

"Shit, here we go again."

They drove through yet another estate at speed, bouncing over several sleeping policemen that had recently been laid to prevent motorists from speeding.

Sara's car bounced over the first one, making her stomach lurch. "How the hell are we going to stop the bastard?"

"We're going to be reliant on the patrol cars helping us. Hopefully, they'll block his path, allowing us to make our move."

"I like your optimism. I think he's more inclined to drive straight through any blockade we set up. We need a miracle to come our way. Hopefully, he'll get a puncture."

"If he doesn't, we probably will before long if we go over many more of those bumps at speed."

Sara laughed, if only to cut through the tension. "Shit, he's put his foot down. He won't be able to sustain this speed for long."

"I'm betting longer than we can."

Sara punched her partner in the leg. "Don't be such a defeatist."

"Do you mind keeping both hands on the steering wheel? It'll be better for my sanity if you did."

"Trust me. I've taken my police pursuit training. You're safe with me."

Carla glanced out of the side window and clenched her hands tightly in her lap. "Whatever. I'm getting married soon, just remember that."

"I've never given you cause to doubt my driving abilities in the past. Why are you giving me grief now?"

"Let's be honest, we've never had to chase a serial killer through housing estates before."

Sara laughed again. "Ha, fair point."

The van left the estate and took a right, which led out into the country again.

"I think we should make our move soon," Sara said.

"What? Are you mad? You'll be putting our lives in danger if you do."

"That's what we signed up for, isn't it? To put our lives on the line daily."

"You might have—I didn't. I was hoping for a cushy desk job when I signed my contract."

Sara tutted. "That's bullshit. I don't believe you."

The van came to a screeching halt and then turned right up a farm track.

"Shit, my suspension is going to be frigging knackered after this."

At the top of the track, the van drove through a gateway which led into one of the farmer's fields. The farmer was in there, herding his flock with three sheepdogs. He raised his fists at Henshaw as he flew past him. Sara lowered her window and shouted an apology as she passed the red-faced farmer.

"Screw you," he shouted back.

"Charming, these country bumpkins, aren't they?"

"Jesus," Carla mumbled beside her. "You and that crazy fucking serial killer ahead of us are tearing up his field. How is he supposed to react, for fuck's sake?"

"All right, calm down. He won't get far now. The gate at the other end of the field will hopefully be closed. He'll have to jump out to open it."

"Either that or he'll ram it open."

Carla's words came true. Henshaw rammed through the farmer's metal gate.

"That'll have done some damage, which might work in our favour."

"You reckon? I can't see him slowing down. Watch out, the gate is bouncing back..." Carla shouted.

The force of the gate connecting with the side of the car knocked it off course. They both hurtled forward with the impact.

Craig stopped behind her and opened the car door. "Are you all right, boss?"

"Yes. Come on, we can't let him get away. Are you all right, Carla?"

She rubbed her head. "I think so."

"Right, we'll go with the boys. I'll come back for the car later."

They unhitched their seat belts and jumped into the back of Craig's car. He put his foot down and caught up with the van.

"Henshaw probably thought he'd seen the last of us. Switch your siren on, Craig. Try to force him off the road."

Beside her, Carla gripped her seat with her eyes closed until her knuckles turned white. Sara had to suppress another laugh.

"Hold tight," Craig shouted.

He eased past the van and immediately pressed his foot on the brake, forcing it to slow down. Henshaw wasn't to be outsmarted. He swerved past them and gave them the finger as he drove by.

"Sorry for screwing up, boss," Craig said.

"You haven't. Don't give up. Seize your opportunity when it arises."

Unfortunately, they were now heading back towards the city. Sara rang the station and gave Jeff their location. "We need to stop him. Now."

"I'll get my team on it, ma'am. Can you stay on the line with me, or are you driving?"

"No, my car is stuck in a field somewhere. I'll collect it later. The four of us are in Craig's vehicle."

Jeff used his radio to contact the patrol cars, making them aware of Sara and her team's location. "My men are out near Morrisons. They've stopped the traffic and are about to put a stinger in place if you can keep the heat up on the suspect, ma'am."

"We'll try. Thanks, Jeff." After several minutes of high-speed pursuit, she said, "We're almost there. Are your men ready?"

"All set up. Keep him coming."

They rounded the corner up ahead, and the van braked sharply. It was too late. The stinger had done its job and pierced all four tyres on the van.

Craig drew the car to a stop and was the first to run towards the vehicle. The other uniformed coppers assisted him. They yanked Henshaw from the driver's seat and forced him to the ground. Craig

had the privilege of slapping the cuffs on him. Sara joined the officers, and when Henshaw was pulled to his feet, she read him his
rights.

"Fuck you. They all deserved it, every last one of them. I would
have completed the task, too, if you hadn't caught me."

Sara grinned. "It's called being on the ball and great detective
work. Take him back to the station and get him processed, Officers."

Henshaw spat at her feet as he was led away.

Sara high-fived Craig, and they walked back to his car. "Can you
take me back to pick up my car?"

"On it now, boss. That turned out to be a satisfactory chase in the
end."

THE TEAM RETURNED to collect Sara's car, which was thankfully still
driveable, and then drove back to the station.

"I'll get the garage to come and pick it up, and then we can start
interviewing the bastard. Jeff has called for the duty solicitor to
attend." Sara waited for Barry to make the coffees and took hers into
her office. She rang her local garage, which told her they would send
a breakdown lorry within the next half an hour.

She drank her coffee while she made some notes for the interview. No doubt Henshaw would be told by the solicitor to go down
the 'no comment' route, but just in case he was eager to get all his
anger off his chest, she filled the page with questions.

Jeff rang her when the duty solicitor arrived. She peered down at
the car park to see the tow lorry pull in. She collected her keys from
her jacket pocket, removed her front door key and headed downstairs
to meet the mechanic.

She passed the solicitor in the reception area. "I'll be with you
soon." She gave the keys to the mechanic and returned to the station.
"If you'd like to come with me, Miss Cavanagh."

The female solicitor picked up her briefcase and followed Sara
down the corridor.

"I'll collect Henshaw so you can have a word with him before we get the interview underway. It would be helpful if you didn't advise him to go down the 'no comment' route."

Miss Cavanagh grinned. "You know as well as I do, Inspector, that isn't going to happen."

"I thought as much. Would you like tea or coffee?"

"Coffee would be wonderful. Thank you."

As Sara walked up the corridor, Carla was nearing the bottom of the stairs.

"I'm going to collect him now," Sara said. "Can you organise the drinks for me? The solicitor wants a coffee. We'll give Henshaw a bottle of water. He won't be able to do much damage with that. Also, can you ask Jeff to help us out with a burly male officer for the interview?"

"Okay. Do you need a hand with him?"

"There should be an officer close by the cells. I'll get them to assist me."

She was right. There was an officer on hand, ready to accompany Henshaw to the interview room. Sara introduced him to his solicitor and left them to get acquainted for the next ten minutes. Carla delivered the drinks and then joined Sara in the reception area. Honouring her word, she texted Lee to inform him that they had arrested someone.

He texted back: *Great team effort.*

Sara replied with a thumbs-up emoji.

Lee responded: *I still need to chat with you. I've uncovered further information. Could do with talking about it in person.*

Sara raised an eyebrow and showed Carla the message.

"Sounds interesting. Unless he's pulling your leg," Carla said.

"I don't know. I think I can trust him." Sara messaged back that she would meet him at three at the same place. "What harm can it do? I've told him I'll meet him later. Back to Henshaw... how did he seem to you?" Sara asked.

"Quiet. Remorseful, maybe."

"Yeah. Not how I expected him to react once he was here. Let's hope he behaves himself during the interview. Are you ready?"

They returned to the interview room.

Henshaw glared at them as they made their way to the table. Sara left Carla to recite the verbiage for the recording.

"Mr Henshaw, or may I call you Alex?" Sara asked.

"Whatever."

"Perhaps you can tell us why you drove off today and sped away like a maniac, trying to escape us?"

He stared at Sara. "No comment."

"Very well. Perhaps you can tell us how you met Oliver Grant?"

"No comment."

"But you admit doing some work at his house this week, yes?"

His lip curled into a faint smile. "No comment."

Sara smirked. "We have video footage of you carrying out work in his house."

He hitched up a shoulder and coughed into his clenched fist. "No comment."

The interview continued in that vein for the next hour. Sara refused to reveal all her cards to Henshaw. She called a halt to the meeting before her anger got the better of her. "We'll interview you again in a few hours. Enjoy your rest."

He grinned and said, "No comment."

Sara asked the officer standing at the back of the room to take him back to his cell. They left the room, and Sara and Carla accompanied the solicitor back to the reception area.

"We'll give you a call later, depending on what turns up in the meantime."

Miss Cavanagh nodded and left the station.

Sara cursed all the way up the stairs. At the top, she peered at her watch. "We've got two hours spare before I have to meet Lee. Do you want to attend the meeting with me?"

"I don't mind. Unless you'd rather go on your own... oh, wait, you need a lift. I knew there was an ulterior motive for you inviting me to a clandestine rendezvous with a journo."

Sara slammed a hand over her chest. "Me? Would I do such a thing?"

"Yes, absolutely."

TWO HOURS LATER, they met Lee at the pub. He was sitting at the bar with a cup and saucer in front of him.

He hadn't seen them enter.

Sara dug him in the ribs. "Nice to see you drinking responsibly in the middle of the day, young man."

Lee twisted on his stool and eyed Carla up and down with appreciation. "Your partner, I take it? We don't see much of you at the conferences, which is a shame. You'd be extremely photogenic in front of the camera."

Sara coughed. "What are you saying? I'm not?"

"Whoa! You're putting words into my mouth," the cocky journalist replied. "Can I get you ladies a drink?"

"Two coffees. I prefer to sit away from the bar. We'll be over here." Sara didn't give him the opportunity to choose a different table.

He placed the order and joined them.

"We haven't got long. We're due to interview the suspect a second time before the end of our shift."

"Fine by me. I've got a list for you." He slid a sheet of paper across the table towards her.

"A list? Is it relevant to our investigation?" Sara asked. She scanned the names briefly and glanced up to see him grinning.

"It might be. Forearmed is to be forewarned, or something like that."

"I believe the saying is the other way around. Who are these people?"

"The others on the committee. Not everyone at those meetings worked for the council."

"Isn't that usually the case?" Sara asked, confused.

"On this occasion, it turns out that Julian Redmond, the committee chair, invited a few of his friends to get involved. And yes, a lot of backhanders were dished out."

"What the fuck?" She read out the names one by one. "Victor Seagrove. Who was he?"

"A council member, or should I say he was retired at the time."

Sara sighed. "Lynda Dobbs?"

"A local historian. She was reluctant to get involved until she found out how much cash they were offering."

Sara shook her head. "Jack Mathers—I recognise that name."

"You should. He was a copper at the time, a notoriously bent one."

"Jesus. Okay, thanks for this. We'll see if we can trace them, if only to get their side of the story."

"I did some extra digging; that's why I wanted to meet with you. Mathers, Dobbs and Seagrove are all dead."

"What? Well, it depends on what age they were when they were on the committee. I suppose twenty years is going to tell with some folks."

"They all died this year. The reason I'm bringing it up is because I don't believe in coincidences."

"Funny that! Neither do I. You believe there's a connection between their deaths and Henshaw going on his killing spree?"

"Possibly. He might have been testing the water. My suggestion would be to check the PM reports and then to ask him about the deaths during an interview, if only to see what his reaction is."

"I'll do that. Again, thanks for the information. I owe you, again," Sara said, genuinely grateful for his help.

"Ah, the four magic words every journalist loves to hear."

Sara rolled her eyes.

"Well, it was nice meeting up with you again, Inspector, and you, Sergeant. Is that an engagement ring I see on your finger?"

"It is. I'm getting married in a couple of weeks—to another detective."

He raised his hands in front of him. "You can't blame a man for chancing his luck."

Sara laughed. "Get out of here. Don't forget to give me an easy time during future conferences."

"I'll have to see about that, won't I?" He winked and left the pub.

"Wow, what do you make of that?" Carla said.

"I'm not surprised he fancies you."

Her partner jabbed her in the side. "Idiot, you know what I was referring to."

"I do. Right, sup up. We need to get back to the station and do some extra digging. I might leave the second interview with Henshaw until the morning. That'll keep him wondering what's going on, won't it?"

"It might be an idea to call Jill and give her the list of names. See what she can find out before we get there," Carla suggested.

Sara was lost deep in thought until Carla nudged her.

"Did you hear what I said?"

"Sorry, yes. You call the station and get the ball rolling there. I'll get in touch with Lorraine, ask her if any of the deaths were suspicious, and if so, I could request the PM reports."

"Makes sense. I need to nip to the loo. I'll give Jill a call on my way."

"Too much information." Sara grinned and dialled Lorraine's number. "Can you talk? It's Sara."

"I'm well aware who it is, and yes, I have ten minutes. What's up?"

"I've been given some names of people who have died this year, and I wanted to run them past you."

"You what? There's got to be a reason why. What is it?"

"Sorry, I should have made you aware of the situation. We've arrested the suspect we've been searching for all week. He's called Alex Henshaw. His family was relocated from an area where the council gave the go-ahead for a shopping complex to be built. We believe he killed the people on a committee involved in the decision —the three victims lying in the fridges at the mortuary. A fourth victim is in hospital after the killer stabbed him. Luckily, the victim's wife interrupted the attack."

"Got that. Congratulations on nailing the bastard. But what's that got to do with these other people?"

"Bear with me. A journalist has furnished me with the names from a file that had been archived at the time. The file had been corrupted, so no one could get their hands on it."

"But your journalist pal managed to get into it, right?"

"Yes, and easy on the pal part. He's a means to an end."

"I was going to ask what was up with you, trusting a journalist. You usually steer clear of them where possible."

"I know. I trust him, especially after the information he has given me. He's the one who led us to the killer in the first place. He did some extra digging and supplied me with this additional evidence. Can I give you the names?"

"Shoot. I'll jot them down as we speak."

Sara did just that. When Lorraine heard each name, she either reacted with a tut or a sigh.

"I take it you recognise the names?"

"I do. Let me check the PM reports first and I'll send them to you."

"Do you think there might have been anything suspicious about the deaths?"

"Possibly. I believe I had niggling doubts about a couple of them. Hard to say off the top of my head. I've probably carried out over a hundred PMs since then, so obviously, things get blurred until I have the information to hand. I'll get back to you soon. Are you thinking this Henshaw killed them?"

"Yes. I believe he might have been perfecting his art before going on his killing spree."

"Gotcha. Sounds plausible. I'll get back to you soon."

"Thanks, Lorraine. I really want to nail this bastard so that he never gets out of prison."

"I can understand that. Leave it with me." Lorraine ended the call.

Sara was still contemplating the magnitude of this extra information when Carla came back from the ladies'.

"How did you get on... er, with Jill, not with...?"

Carla tutted and shook her head. "I knew what you meant. She's going to get the team on it now."

"Great. Lorraine is checking the PM reports."

"Did you tell her?"

"Yep, of course. She said that a couple of them might have been suspicious deaths at the time, but there was nothing concrete about them."

"Helpful. Should we get back now?"

"Let's finish our drinks first." She picked up her phone again and rang the desk sergeant. "Hi, Jeff. It's Sara Ramsey. I won't be interviewing Henshaw again tonight. We've uncovered some fresh evidence that we need to go over before I tackle him."

"Sounds intriguing. Okay, I'll make him comfortable for the evening."

"Thanks. Don't tell him anything, though. Let's keep him wondering what the hell is going on."

He laughed. "My thoughts exactly."

"We'll be back soon." Sara placed her phone back on the table and finished her coffee. "It's been an eventful day so far and it's not over yet."

"What about Lawton? Should you call the hospital now, to check what his status is?"

"Damn. I knew there was something else I had to do." She rang the hospital to be told he was in surgery. "Thanks, will you let Mrs Lawton know that I rang?"

"I'll do that. She's sitting in the reception area with me."

"Take care of her for us. I'll have some good news for her when I see her again."

"Do you want me to pass that message on to her? She looks down in the mouth; some good news might raise her spirits."

"Go on then. Tell her we've caught the suspect."

"Oh, she will be pleased to hear that. Well done, Inspector."

"It was teamwork. Thank you. Send her my best wishes and tell her I'll be in touch in the next day or two."

"I'll do that."

Sara slipped her phone into her pocket, rubbed at her eyes and let out a yawn. "Jesus, I'm cream crackered, not something you'll hear me say that often."

"It's been a hell of a day. The good news is that it's ending better than it started."

"You're not wrong there. Come on, let's get back to the grind for the final push. We're almost there now."

# EPILOGUE

On their way back to the station, Carla and Sara called at Henshaw's house. His mother opened the door. She seemed frail and shocked to see them. She invited them in and flopped into the armchair in the lounge.

"I'm sorry. I can't stand for long. I've just completed chemo, and it has thoroughly drained me."

"So sorry to hear that, Mrs Henshaw."

"It is what it is. It was a last resort. The consultant wants to see me tomorrow. I'm judging by his tone over the phone that the news isn't the best. Never mind, I've lived my life. It's not always been easy, especially since Ian left me."

"Is that your husband?"

"Yes. He committed suicide eighteen years ago."

"Oh no, that's tragic. Sorry for your loss."

Tears welled up in her eyes. "Like I said, it hasn't always been easy bringing up Alex on my own. I had no skills behind me; therefore, I was forced to take on cleaning jobs that worked around my son's education."

"He's an electrician, isn't he?" Sara asked. Her aim was to get as much information out of his mother before she revealed why they were there.

"He is. I'm so proud of him. He's not long started up on his own."

"Has he found much work since starting up?"

"Oh yes. He's been nonstop since the day he bought his van. He's saving up to get it sign-written. Is that what they call it?"

Sara smiled and nodded. "I believe that's correct. Are you close to him?"

"Yes. The cancer has been an issue between us. I think the thought of losing me, as well as his father, has hit him harder than either of us could have imagined."

"It's not pleasant to deal with. I'm speaking from experience. When you hear the terrible statistics they're bandying about at the moment, I don't think any family will escape it."

"I know. You'd think that with the amount of money that has gone into researching the disease, they'd have found a cure for it by now."

"I agree. What sort of character is your son?"

Mrs Henshaw frowned. "Hmm... how would I describe him? That's a good question. I suppose he's always been a bit of a loner, devoted to me and his father when he was alive."

"That's nice to hear. So, he didn't have many friends growing up?"

"Not really. Boys tended to look down on kids from one-parent families when he was at school. He was bullied a fair bit. He didn't tell me. I found out via the head at the school. I sat him down and tried to get the information out of him, but he refused to confide in me and went into his shell. This was when he was thirteen. I suppose he remained in his shell until he started his apprenticeship."

"And then he was all right about mixing with people, was he?"

"I think so. He's never been very open with his feelings, otherwise he would have told me he was being bullied at school. Sorry, but why are you here, asking about my son? I should have asked you at the door before I let you in, but my legs were wobbling, and I was desperate to sit down."

*Crunch time!* "It is with regret that I have to inform you that your son has been arrested."

The confusion increased in her features. Her brow furrowed deeply, and her gaze darted between them. "What? Why? He's never broken the law, not that I know of. Are you sure you haven't made a mistake?"

"I'm sorry, but the evidence we have on your son is pretty solid. We're going to need to get a warrant to search his room, unless you're willing to let us have a quick look now, while we're here?"

"Of course, if it'll help prove his innocence. What's he been charged with?" Mrs Henshaw dipped into her handbag and removed an inhaler. "I have asthma, and I'm struggling to breathe."

"Take your time. Can we call anyone to come and sit with you?"

"My neighbour, Shirley."

"Right or left?" Sara asked, the panic rising within.

"Right." She took another couple of puffs from the inhaler.

Sara shot out of her chair and raced outside. She knocked on the house next door. Thankfully, it was opened within seconds by an elderly woman around the same age as Mrs Henshaw.

Sara produced her ID. "Can you come and sit with Mrs Henshaw for a while? She's having an asthma attack."

"Oh my, yes. I'll get my key."

Sara returned to the lounge; she left the front door open so that Shirley could join them.

"Nell, my God, are you all right, love?" Shirley ran over to Nell and knelt beside her. "How did this happen? You haven't had an attack in years."

"I can answer that. We've just delivered some shocking news that Nell hasn't taken well," Sara informed her.

"Nell, what's wrong?"

"They've arrested Alex. I don't know what for; they haven't got around to telling me," she said in between gasps for breath.

"I'd rather not cause you any further distress. Will you allow us to search his bedroom?"

"That doesn't sound good. She needs to know," Shirley insisted.

"Yes, please tell me," Nell pleaded. She clutched her friend's hand for support.

"We believe he's killed several people in the community this week, maybe more over the past few months."

"What? No! That can't be true," Nell shouted. She inhaled another couple of puffs, and Shirley threw an arm around her shoulder.

"Let them do the necessary searches, love, if it'll prove his innocence," Shirley advised.

"Thank you. Does he have an office here as well?"

"Yes. He uses the dining room; it's a bit of a mess in there."

"Don't worry. We're eager to find his diary. Do you know where that is?"

"It's on the dining room table. If it's not there, it could be in his van," Nell replied. "I can't believe any of this is true of Alex. He wouldn't deliberately set out to harm anyone, he just wouldn't."

Sara and Carla left the neighbours and wandered down the hallway to the dining room.

"You search that side," Sara said.

They snapped on a pair of gloves each before they started.

Together, they made short work of the task. Buried beneath a pile of bills, Sara found his diary. She skimmed through previous months and located the names she was looking for.

"This is all the proof we need. We'll ask her if we can take it with us."

"Is she going to be all right? I don't think I could handle another trip to the hospital this week," Carla asked.

"I'm sure she'll be fine. Shirley seems to have it all in hand. Maybe she has medical training under her belt."

They returned to the lounge.

"How are you feeling now, Nell?" Sara asked.

"I'm all right. Well, sort of... Did you find what you were looking for?"

Sara held up the diary, which she had already put in an evidence bag. "I have. Do we have your permission to take it?"

"Yes. Do what you have to. What about Alex? Can I see him?"

"Not yet. We have to interview him first. That'll take place tomorrow. He'll be charged and sent on remand. You'll be able to visit him once he's been transferred."

Nell nodded, then covered her face with her hands and sobbed. "This can't be happening, not to my son."

"We have to go now. Please, take care of yourself. I'll leave my card on the hall table for you. Call me if you need to, okay?"

Shirley nodded. "Thank you. I'll take care of her."

Sara smiled, then she and Carla left the house and drove back to the station.


THE FOLLOWING MORNING, with the fresh evidence they had gathered to hand, they interviewed Alex Henshaw again. Miss Cavanagh joined them as the duty solicitor.

Sara pulled her trump card and placed her hand on Henshaw's work diary. "As you can see, we have your diary to hand, Alex. Your mother was kind enough to allow us access to your temporary office."

"What? Can they do that? Badger my mother like that?" he asked Cavanagh.

Before the solicitor could respond, Sara said, "We didn't badger her. She was very forthcoming with us and told us what you went through at school, the bullying you had to contend with during your teens. She also told us that you lost your father eighteen years ago. Did his death affect you?"

He glared at Sara, and she expected him to reply, 'No comment', but he didn't.

Instead, he snarled, "What do you think?"

"Why now? Why set out to kill the people on that committee now?" Sara had an inkling, but she'd rather get the facts from the suspect.

He shook his head, and his gaze dropped to his clenched hands. "It's because of what's happening with my mother."

"I thought as much. You're scared of losing her as well, is that right?"

He nodded. "Those people deserved to die. They drove my father to commit suicide. The house we were moved to wasn't up to much. It was damp and cold. Mum didn't have the funds to carry out the maintenance on it. I've done my best over the past few years to address the situation, but it couldn't prevent her from getting cancer. Now that's going to kill her. You saw how frail she is. The chemo has taken a lot out of her…"

"You need to stay positive. Your mother told us that she has to see the consultant in a few days. It could be good news."

"She doesn't seem to think so. I wanted her to be proud of me before she went. I wanted her to know that I had punished all those who had put us through hell over the years. It doesn't matter to me that I will spend the rest of my life in prison; once she's gone, I'll have nothing left anyway."

"You're wrong. From what we can see, you have a thriving business to pursue."

"I made it a success so that I could pay Mum back for raising me single-handedly without any help from government handouts. There were days when she went without food, just so I could have a piece of bread in my stomach. Once the bullying started, it got me thinking about all those people who had lined their pockets to build that complex, not giving a stuff about the families they cast aside. I had to right those wrongs. I don't regret killing them, either. I'll sign a statement now, admitting to every murder that I've committed this week."

"And what about the others you've killed this year?"

"Yes, and them. I'll confess to all of them. Please look after my mother for me. She deserves to be treated well in the time she has left on Earth."

"Don't worry. I'll ensure she's well cared for. We'll get the statement written up and then transfer you to the remand centre. Your mother will be able to visit you there."

"Thank you. I repeat: I have no regrets and feel no remorse. The fuckers deserved to die. I'm just sorry it took me so long to deal with the issue."

"Thank you for your honesty. Constable, take Mr Henshaw back to his cell."

The two men left the room.

Sara accompanied Miss Cavanagh back to the reception area and shook her hand. "We got the truth out of him in the end."

"I'm glad," Miss Cavanagh said, then turned and walked out of the station.

On the way back to the incident room, instead of feeling jubilant, Sara felt like the wind had been knocked out of her sails.

"Hey, why are you so glum?" Carla asked.

"Because sometimes justice isn't a satisfactory ending to the problem."

"Hmm... I never thought about it that way before. You're right. Will there be an enquiry now, naming and shaming all those who illegally took backhanders?"

"Absolutely. We'll hand over all our evidence. Someone else can deal with that onerous task."

"I agree. We've done the hard work; someone else can pick up the slack now. Fancy a coffee?"

"Nope. I need to go home, hug my husband and tell him how much I love him. You should do the same to Des. You have a good man there, Carla."

"I know, that's why I'm marrying him."

"You two were suited from the day you met. You should also visit your father. He should have had his operation today, shouldn't he?"

"Yes. I'll do that. We still need to have a discussion about what went on twenty years ago. I'm not sure I'll ever be able to forgive him for what he put those people through."

"You will. You have to. He might have been riddled with guilt all these years."

"We'll see. Thanks for understanding, Sara."

"That's what friends are for." They hugged. "We make a great team, don't ever forget that."

"You're not wrong."

THE END

. . .

THANK you for reading Shadows of Deception, don't miss the next thrilling adventure in this series, The Killing Route

While I have your attention, have you read any of my other fast-paced crime thrillers yet?

WHY NOT TRY the first book in the award-winning Justice series, the first book is Cruel Justice

OR THE FIRST book in the spin-off Justice Again series,
Gone in Seconds

MAYBE YOU'D PREFER my thriller series set in the stunning Lake District, the first book is To Die For

PERHAPS YOU'D PREFER to try one of my other police procedural series, the DI Kayli Bright series which begins with
The Missing Children

OR MAYBE YOU'D enjoy the DI Sally Parker series set in Norfolk,
Wrong Place

OR MY GRITTY police procedural starring DI Nelson set in Manchester, Torn Apart

OR MAYBE YOU'D like to try one of my successful psychological thrillers I know The Truth or She's Gone or Shattered Lives

# KEEP IN TOUCH WITH M A COMLEY

Newsletter
http://smarturl.it/8jtcvv

BookBub
www.bookbub.com/authors/m-a-comley

Blog
http://melcomley.blogspot.com

Facebook Readers' Page
https://www.facebook.com/groups/2498593423507951

TikTok
https://www.tiktok.com/@melcomley

# ALSO BY M A COMLEY

Blind Justice (Novella)

Cruel Justice (Book #1)

Mortal Justice (Novella)

Impeding Justice (Book #2)

Final Justice (Book #3)

Foul Justice (Book #4)

Guaranteed Justice (Book #5)

Ultimate Justice (Book #6)

Virtual Justice (Book #7)

Hostile Justice (Book #8)

Tortured Justice (Book #9)

Rough Justice (Book #10)

Dubious Justice (Book #11)

Calculated Justice (Book #12)

Twisted Justice (Book #13)

Justice at Christmas (Short Story)

Prime Justice (Book #14)

Heroic Justice (Book #15)

Shameful Justice (Book #16)

Immoral Justice (Book #17)

Toxic Justice (Book #18)

Overdue Justice (Book #19)

Unfair Justice (a 10,000 word short story)

Irrational Justice (a 10,000 word short story)

Wrong Place (DI Sally Parker thriller #1)

No Hiding Place (DI Sally Parker thriller #2)

Cold Case (DI Sally Parker thriller#3)

Deadly Encounter (DI Sally Parker thriller #4)

Lost Innocence (DI Sally Parker thriller #5)

Goodbye My Precious Child (DI Sally Parker #6)

The Missing Wife (DI Sally Parker #7)

Truth or Dare (DI Sally Parker #8)

Where Did She Go? (DI Sally Parker #9)

Sinner (DI Sally Parker #10)

The Good Die Young (DI Sally Parker#11)

Coping Without You (DI Sally Parker #12)

Could It Be Him (DI Sally Parker #13)

Frozen In Time (DI Sally Parker #14)

Echoes of Silence (DI Sally Parker #15)

The Final Betrayal (DI Sally Parker #16)

Garden of Bones (DI Sally Parker #17)

Web of Deceit (DI Sally Parker Novella)

The Missing Children (DI Kayli Bright #1)

Killer On The Run (DI Kayli Bright #2)

Hidden Agenda (DI Kayli Bright #3)

Murderous Betrayal (Kayli Bright #4)

Dying Breath (Kayli Bright #5)

Taken (DI Kayli Bright #6)

The Hostage Takers (DI Kayli Bright Novella)

No Right to Kill (DI Sara Ramsey #1)

Killer Blow (DI Sara Ramsey #2)

The Dead Can't Speak (DI Sara Ramsey #3)

Deluded (DI Sara Ramsey #4)

The Murder Pact (DI Sara Ramsey #5)

Twisted Revenge (DI Sara Ramsey #6)

The Lies She Told (DI Sara Ramsey #7)

For The Love Of... (DI Sara Ramsey #8)

Run for Your Life (DI Sara Ramsey #9)

Cold Mercy (DI Sara Ramsey #10)

Sign of Evil (DI Sara Ramsey #11)

Indefensible (DI Sara Ramsey #12)

Locked Away (DI Sara Ramsey #13)

I Can See You (DI Sara Ramsey #14)

The Kill List (DI Sara Ramsey #15)

Crossing The Line (DI Sara Ramsey #16)

Time to Kill (DI Sara Ramsey #17)

Deadly Passion (DI Sara Ramsey #18)

Son of the Dead (DI Sara Ramsey #19)

Evil Intent (DI Sara Ramsey #20)

The Games People Play (DI Sara Ramsey #21)

Revenge Streak (DI Sara Ramsey #22)

Seeking Retribution (DI Sara Ramsey #23)

Gone... But Where? (DI Sara Ramsey #24)

Last Man Standing (DI Sara Ramsey #25)

Vanished (DI Sara Ramsey #26)

Shadows of Deception (DI Sara Ramsey #27)

The Killing Route (DI Sara Ramsey #28)

I Know The Truth (A Psychological thriller)

She's Gone (A psychological thriller)

Shattered Lives (A psychological thriller)

Evil In Disguise – a novel based on True events

Deadly Act (Hero series novella)

Torn Apart (Hero series #1)

End Result (Hero series #2)

In Plain Sight (Hero Series #3)

Double Jeopardy (Hero Series #4)

Criminal Actions (Hero Series #5)

Regrets Mean Nothing (Hero series #6)

Prowlers (Di Hero Series #7)

Sole Intention (Intention series #1)

Grave Intention (Intention series #2)

Devious Intention (Intention #3)

Cozy mysteries

Murder at the Wedding

Murder at the Hotel

Murder by the Sea

Death on the Coast

Death By Association

Merry Widow (A Lorne Simpkins short story)

It's A Dog's Life (A Lorne Simpkins short story)

A Time To Heal (A Sweet Romance)

A Time For Change (A Sweet Romance)

High Spirits

The Temptation series (Romantic Suspense/New Adult Novellas)

Past Temptation

Lost Temptation

Printed in Dunstable, United Kingdom

63647192R00117